OUR POISONED SKY

■ □ ■

OUR POISONED SKY

EDWARD F. DOLAN

Illustrated with photographs and diagrams

COBBLEHILL BOOKS
Dutton   New York

Diagrams by Werner Desepte

Copyright © 1991 by Edward F. Dolan
All rights reserved
No part of this book may be reproduced in any form
without permission in writing from the publisher.

Library of Congress Cataloging-in-Publication Data
Dolan, Edward F., date
    Our poisoned sky / Edward F. Dolan.
      p.   cm.
    Includes bibliographical references and index.
    Summary: Explains how pollutants are ruining our atmosphere
and what is being done about them.
    ISBN 0-525-65056-3
    1. Air—Pollution—Juvenile literature.   [1. Air—Pollution.
2. Pollution.]   I. Title.
TD883.13.D65   1991   363.73'92—dc20   90-14031   CIP   AC

Published in the United States by Cobblehill Books,
an affiliate of Dutton Children's Books, a division
of Penguin Books USA Inc.
375 Hudson Street, New York, New York 10014
Designed by Mina Greenstein
Printed in the United States of America
First Edition   10 9 8 7 6 5 4 3 2

CONTENTS

1 ·	Our Poisoned Sky	1
2 ·	The Poisons: Pollutants Identified	10
3 ·	The Ozone Layer: Holes in the Sky	24
4 ·	Acid Rain: "Death from the Sky"	39
5 ·	The Greenhouse Effect: A Dangerous Heat	56
6 ·	Fighting Pollutants: The Worldwide Effort	70
7 ·	Fighting Pollutants: The American Effort	81
8 ·	What About the Other Major Problems?	94
9 ·	What You Can Do to Help	106
	Bibliography	113
	Index	119

OUR POISONED SKY

1

OUR POISONED SKY

December 6: For three days now, a thick smog has held London, England, in its choking grip. Dark and evil-smelling, it is made up chiefly of the smoke and ashes that pour from the coal being burned in the city's factories, shops, and home fireplaces. People wear gauze surgical masks as they struggle through their daily lives and wait for the return of the wind that has always blown the stuff away in the past. The hospitals fill with patients suffering complaints that range from wheezing and coughing to severe breathing problems and—because of the physical strain that goes with fighting for breath—heart ailments. A wind rises at last on December 10 and clears the air. But the smog has taken 4,000 lives. Another 8,000 people will die in the next weeks as a result of the ordeal.

2 ■ OUR POISONED SKY

■

What is now remembered as "London's killer smog" struck the city some forty years ago, in 1952. To this day, it stands as a reminder of just how deadly it can be to pollute the air as our country and its fellow industrialized nations are doing every day of the week. But it does not stand alone in warning us of the consequences of this daily poisoning of the atmosphere. It is joined by many other stories. For example:

> On a night in the 1960s, there is a delay as drivers are leaving a crowded indoor car park in Boston. Fumes from the exhaust pipes of the idling cars turn the air gray. Soon, people are sick with nausea. Some are choking. Others are fainting. The delay has been caused by the cars stopping at the exit to pay their parking fees. An attendant recognizes the cause of the trouble—the carbon monoxide in the exhaust fumes. Death, he knows, can come in mere minutes. He quickly clears the place by letting the cars leave without stopping at the pay booth. His action saves the lives of everyone. But more than twenty-five people have to be hospitalized for carbon monoxide poisoning.

■

Frightening news comes from Antarctica in 1985. Scientists report that, for several years, a giant hole has been appearing in the ozone layer high above the frozen continent. The layer—which is named for the gas, ozone—shields the world from the sun's harmful ultraviolet radiation. If the hole marks the start of a widespread breakup of the layer, the results can be disastrous. The growing amount of ultraviolet radiation that will then reach the earth can lead to an increase in certain illnesses, among them skin cancers. It can also lead to a global food shortage by stunting the growth of plants and animals. Researchers blame the Antarctic hole on a number of man-made gases—the chlorofluorocarbons (CFCs). They are used worldwide in such products as refrigerators, air conditioners, and insulation materials.

■

The 1970s bring word of an odd rain that is falling on parts of the United States and Canada. Christened *acid rain* by the media, it is soon being seen in western Europe. Research shows that it is damaging forests and so polluting lakes and streams that their fish are dying. Charged with being at fault are the sulfur and nitrogen in the smoke coming from coal-burning electric power plants and factories.

■

The 1970s also bring word that the world's climate seems to be embarked on a warming trend. Scientists warn that a number of gases here on earth—among them, the carbon dioxide found in factory, home, and other smoke—are contributing to the suspected warming trend in a phenomenon known as the *greenhouse effect*. These gases, in concert with the growing warmth, can lead to extensive droughts that will result in global crop losses and starvation. There can also be a melting of the world's glaciers, a melting that is viewed as catastrophic because it will raise ocean levels, alter present-day coastlines everywhere, and possibly cause the loss of important harbors and seaside towns.

■

Atmospheric pollution is called one of the greatest environmental dangers that we face in today's industrialized world. We humans are also polluting our lands and waters, but atmospheric pollution may well pose the greatest danger of all because it threatens the air that we must breathe to survive. Take that air away and life ends.

This is exactly what the people of the world are doing today—taking the air away by smothering it with the poisons that spew from our smokestacks, car and aircraft exhaust systems, and the chemicals that we have devised for use in a staggering array of products. We have so poisoned the sky that we are now endangering our health (and that of all our fellow living beings, plants and animals alike) and reducing our enjoyment of life by having to live with the stench of gasoline fumes and the filthy yellow haze that is smog. There is a growing fear worldwide that, unless the harm is stopped, we may eventually destroy all life on our planet.

Everyone of us is aware of today's air pollution. Smog and acid rain have become household words throughout the world. News reports of such dangers as the greenhouse effect and the shredding of the ozone layer are commonplace. But it is one thing to be aware of a problem, and another to know its causes, its true extent, and what must be done to end it. To help you understand exactly what is happening to our atmosphere and to help you see what is being done to correct the harm—and what each of us can do to help—is the purpose of this book.

WHEN DID IT ALL BEGIN?

Work is completed on the new copper smelting plant at Copper Basin, Tennessee, early in the year. Smoke begins to pour daily from the plant chimneys and rolls out over the surrounding lands. It silently destroys some 15,000 acres of crop plantings and more than 30,000 acres of timberland. The land will remain barren for years to come.

■

The people of Pittsburgh, Pennsylvania, are angry. They breathe an air so smoky that they are forced to live with constantly wrinkled noses and watery eyes. At last, no longer able to tolerate the problem, they demand that the city government take action. Pittsburgh enacts its first smoke abatement laws.

■

The members of England's governing body, Parliament, are as angry as the people of Pittsburgh. The London sky is so filled with smoke from coal-burning home fireplaces that they cannot go about their business without choking and sneezing. They decide on a drastic action. They enact legislation that forbids everyone in the city from lighting a coal fire while Parliament is in session.

■

Do these stories sound as if they come from today's newspapers and television newscasts? They may indeed sound that way, but such is not the case. The Tennessee smelting plant did its harm in the late 1860s, the years immediately following the Civil War. The angry cries for action in Pittsburgh were heard at an even earlier date—1812.

And what of that law forbidding the burning of coal in London while Parliament was in session? It was passed more than 600 years ago—in 1306. An old story has it that a man was hanged for disobeying the edict.

While air pollution is especially menacing today, there is nothing new about it. As the above stories prove, it has been with us for a long while. The fact is, it has been around since the dawn of time when the first brush and forest fires sent clouds of smoke billowing skyward. It grew when we humans harnessed fire and began to use it for warmth and cooking. It grew still more when we built houses, stores, workshops, and public buildings and equipped them with fireplaces and chimneys.

And it dates back to the very beginning of life on our planet—back to the first appearance of the bacteria, plants, insects, and animals that give off such gases as methane, which joins carbon dioxide in playing a role in today's greenhouse effect. And back to the very first moment when the winds sent dust and bits of soil swirling into the air. And back to the birth of the lightning flashes that create so much ozone, the gas that is seen today as both helpful and dangerous to us. It is helpful because, on rising into the stratosphere, ozone has the ability to hold back most of the sun's ultraviolet radiation—a radiation that can harm all living things if received in too great a quantity. But ozone turns dangerous when present down here on earth. It becomes one of the most treacherous and health-threatening pollutants in smog. Many scientists think it is *the* most treacherous of all the elements that make up smog.

Though air pollution has been with us for eons, it did

not become a danger to our planet until a little over two centuries ago. Before that time, the atmosphere was able to handle the pollutants that came from natural and manmade fires and from the gases emitted by plant and animal life. Vast as it was—and is—it absorbed some of their number. It neutralized others. It put still others, such as ozone, to useful work. In all, nature was in balance in the sky. Today, that balance has been upset, with results that promise to be devastating.

Every story in this chapter makes it painfully clear that we humans are to blame for throwing nature in the sky out of kilter. What we have done is add so many pollutants of our making to those that have been there for eons that the atmosphere is no longer able to handle them all. Since we are at fault for the trouble—and since we are the only creatures on the planet who are able to recognize the problem—we must take the responsibility for getting rid of it.

But how exactly did all this harm come about?

THE INDUSTRIAL REVOLUTION

The answer begins close to 250 years ago with the birth of the Industrial Age in eighteenth-century England. Previously, agriculture had been the nation's principal business. But now factories began to cover the fields where crops had once grown. Cities took shape as more and more people settled around the factories where jobs were to be had. To power the factories, the British began to burn coal, the fossil fuel that had hitherto been used mostly for warmth. In the murky clouds that poured from the increasing number of smokestacks came the pollutants that are born when coal is burned. And out of the chimneys that rose like brick forests from the homes in the growing cities came the same poisons. Soon, these pollutants were choking the air—and the people—of England's first industrial centers. The burning of coal in the homes of London had bothered Parliament back in 1306. Now the smoke was thicker than ever before.

Matters worsened as the Industrial Revolution spread across the world. They worsened further when the burning of coal was joined by the burning of its two fellow fossil fuels—oil and natural gas. They continue to worsen today as we go on powering our factories and electric utility plants with the fossil fuels. We've added to the trouble with the major developments of the past one hundred years—to name two of the worst, the invention of the gasoline (internal combustion) engine and the invention of chemical compounds for use in a seemingly endless array of commercial products.

FOUR PROBLEMS

In all, the poisons that we humans have unleashed into the air have given us four problems—problems that, with the spread of the Industrial Revolution for well over the past 200 years, are now suffered worldwide. They are problems that are endangering all life on our planet—and problems that are placing a heavy economic burden on many nations. Here in the United States, according to an estimate by the American Lung Association, the health damage that they wreak is costing the people upwards of $40 billion a year for medical care and time lost on the job. These four major problems are:

1. Our industries, our gasoline engines, and the chemicals used in many of our modern products have loosed *pollutants* that, in themselves, have the power to sicken and kill. Some of their number play a role in the formation of smog, which, likewise, has the power to sicken and kill.

2. The industrial burning of the fossil fuels, especially the burning of coal, has given us *acid rain*.

3. These same burnings are contributing to the *greenhouse effect*. In its turn, the greenhouse effect is contributing to the dangerous warming trend on which, in the view of many scientists, the world's climate is now embarked.

4. The man-made chemical compounds known as the *chlorofluorocarbons* (CFCs) are shredding the ozone layer and leaving us increasingly exposed to the dangers of the sun's ultraviolet radiation.

These four worldwide problems—and the pollutants totally or in part responsible for them—are to be the subjects of this book. While the dangers they pose for us are many and grave, our situation is not hopeless. The dangers can be eased or eliminated if firm actions are taken against them. Fortunately, as we shall see, many such actions are already being taken by the nations of the world—though many more that are desperately needed have so far gone ignored. And, happily, as we shall also see, there are many things that each of us can do as individuals to help make our poisoned sky the fresh and clean expanse of blue it once was.

2

■ □ ■

THE POISONS
Pollutants Identified

The pollutants that, singly or in some combination, have the power to sicken and even kill can be divided into five general categories. We are going to look at them each in turn. They are:

The carbon pollutants
Suspended particulate matter
The sulfur oxides and nitrogen oxides
Toxic substances
The pollutants in smog

THE CARBON POLLUTANTS

Carbon is one of the most common elements found in nature. It is present in a wide variety of substances that range from coal, oil, and graphite to limestone, diamonds, and a number of organic compounds. It is also the producer of two of the most damaging pollutants in the atmosphere—carbon monoxide and the hydrocarbons.

Carbon Monoxide

Described as a colorless, odorless, and tasteless gas, carbon monoxide takes shape when a carbon fuel is incompletely burned. The greatest producer of this gas is the gasoline engine. Carbon monoxide is especially prevalent in crowded urban areas, where heavy traffic results in stop-and-go driving. The irregular movement causes your car engine to perform less efficiently (namely, causes the explosions generated by the piston strokes to fail to burn away all the fuel in the cylinders) than is the case when you are traveling at a steady pace. The result is that the unburned fuel transforms itself into carbon monoxide and is released into the atmosphere as fumes via the car's exhaust system.

But the gasoline engine, while chiefly to blame, is not solely at fault for the high concentration of carbon monoxide in today's atmosphere. Aircraft and industrial operations such as steel plants and smelters also produce the gas.

Carbon monoxide is a poisonous gas. It is at its most dangerous when it gathers in a confined, enclosed space, such as the Boston indoor parking garage that was mentioned in Chapter 1. On being inhaled, it attacks the life-giving oxygen in the bloodstream and reduces the amount of oxygen that is being carried to parts of the body. When the oxygen is too far reduced, carbon monoxide poisoning results and can quickly bring death.

Only one part carbon monoxide to 100,000 parts of other substances in the air can induce carbon monoxide poisoning in a matter of minutes. The symptoms of the poisoning usually begin with headache, nausea, muscular weakness, and the development of a cherry-red color to the skin. They then advance to the impairment of the thinking process, unconsciousness, and finally death. Death can come in about a half hour when there is one part carbon monoxide to 750 parts of other substances in the air.

There is only one cure for carbon monoxide poisoning—the return of sufficient oxygen to the bloodstream. Fast action is needed to save its victims. They must be rushed into the fresh air. If not breathing, they should be given artificial respiration. If possible to do so, it is best to administer the artificial respiration with an inhalator and pure oxygen.

For many years, carbon monoxide was not considered a major outdoor hazard. Scientists thought that the atmosphere gave it plenty of space in which to dissipate. But now, with cities choked with its fumes, there has been a change of mind. The gas may not be the killer that it is in an enclosed space, but it is nevertheless seen as posing certain health threats.

For one, medical research indicates that there is such a disorder as chronic carbon monoxide poisoning. Caused by the daily inhalation of the fumes—especially those from car exhaust systems—it presents in milder form the same symptoms that are seen in acute cases of the poisoning—dizziness, nausea, headache, and physical weakness, all caused by a loss of oxygen in the bloodstream. While chronic carbon monoxide poisoning does not kill, some scientists believe it to be at fault in many traffic accidents that are attributed to driver tiredness.

Physicians also point out that carbon monoxide in the outdoors poses a threat for people who suffer or are prone to heart and lung problems. Again at fault is that loss of oxygen. The heart and lungs are forced to overwork in its absence. Studies at the University of California suggest that automobile fumes may cause up to 30,000 American deaths annually.

Hydrocarbons

Hydrocarbons are gaseous compounds that are made up of carbon and hydrogen. Like carbon monoxide, they are born when there is an incomplete burning of carbon fuels. They are mostly emitted from gasoline engines, stoves, home and industrial furnaces, and gasoline and diesel service stations. Consequently, as can be expected, they gather in their greatest concentrations in urban and industrial areas where automobile use is widespread.

Most hydrocarbons, at the levels found in the atmosphere, are not poisonous. But there are several types that are known to be carcinogens—meaning they cause cancer—if one is exposed to them for too long a time; one particularly dangerous type is the gas hemozoprine. The greatest fear concerning the hydrocarbons, however, centers on the role they play in the formation of smog.

SUSPENDED PARTICULATE MATTER

As its name indicates, suspended particulate matter consists of the particles that are emitted from various natural and man-made sources and then make their contribution to pollution by hanging suspended in the air. The particles, which can be in either liquid or solid form, range in size from those bits-and-pieces that are visible as dust, sand, grit, and soot to those that are so minute that they can be seen only with the aid of an electron microscope.

Beyond count in number, the particles are found everywhere. They make up the dust and pollens that the winds send whirling into the air. They rise from every load of coal that is mined, and from the industrial plants that refine or use oil. They pour from the factories that produce cement. In fact, they come from every industrial installation that sends smoke up through its stacks. And they are spewed daily from automobile exhaust systems.

Small as they may be, the particles add up to billions of tons of air pollution worldwide. Only one example is needed to prove how much their total weight can run. Some years ago, a research study found that a single industry in Chicago produced more than 10,000 tons of particulate matter each day of its operation.

At their least, the particles are a nuisance as they settle on our buildings, streets, and car windshields. At their worst, they are distinct health hazards. Some trigger allergies. The inhalation of coal and stone dust is known to result in pneumoconiosis (or, as it is more commonly called, silicosis), the lung disease that strikes coal miners and quarry workers. Many doctors suspect there is a connection between the constantly rising soot content in the atmosphere and the growing number of pneumonia cases that have been reported in various areas during recent years. Also identified as dangerous are the particles in the additives—tetraethyl lead, chlorine, and bromine—that have long been injected into gasoline to make the automobile engine work more efficiently. Medical research indicates that they can hinder the body's ability to produce red blood cells. Red blood cells carry oxygen throughout the body.

Some of the most dangerous particles are found in one the most commonly used of all modern products—asbestos. Admired worldwide because it does not burn, asbestos has served for decades as a fireproofing agent in a host of products—paints, cements, plastics, clothes, automobile brake linings, and such everyday household items as pot holders and ironing board covers. In one of its most popular uses, it has gone into the wall and roofing materials employed in home and building construction.

Though an excellent safeguard against fire, asbestos can raise havoc when the particles in it escape into the air during its manufacture and whenever asbestos-walled structures are torn down, car braking systems wear out, and various household appliances give out. Prolonged exposure to the particles can result in asbestosis, a disease that, like pneumoconiosis, attacks the lungs. The victims of the disease are usually workers in plants manufacturing asbestos. Even when inhalation is not prolonged, the particles can induce the lung cancer known as mesothelioma. It is a type of cancer that is almost always associated with asbestos dust.

SULFUR AND NITROGEN OXIDES

As their names make clear, each of these oxides is made up of substances containing either sulfur or nitrogen. They are created together when a fuel containing both sulfur and nitrogen—such as coal or oil—is burned. Each of the two produces it own oxide molecules on mixing with the oxygen in the air.

The heaviest sulfur and nitrogen emissions in the United States come from factories and electric power plants that burn coal and from the gasoline engine. As a consequence, of course, the emissions are at their worst in regions that are industrialized and densely populated and have a high concentration of automobiles.

One type of sulfur oxide—sulfur dioxide—ranks as a particular health menace. It attacks the lungs and can cause the lung inflammation called emphysema. It can also irritate the skin and eyes, and is thought to be a principal cause of catarrh, an inflammation that usually strikes the air passages in the head and throat.

Nitrogen oxide, for its part, can turn into nitric acid, which is especially dangerous because it attacks the body as carbon monoxide does; it reduces the oxygen content traveling through the bloodstream. Another nitrogen product—nitrogen dioxide—can damage the lungs if inhaled in sufficient quantity.

Both sulfur and nitrogen, as we will see later, combine to give us acid rain. Nitrogen also plays a role in the creation of smog.

TOXIC SUBSTANCES

Toxic substances are described as pollutants that harm living beings or alter the environment in ways that cause the death of plants and animals. Much the same description can be applied to the other pollutants we have discussed thus far. But there is a difference. For the most part, the other pollutants result from burnings. Toxic substances do not.

The list of toxic substances is long and varied. High on the list are the pesticides used to kill insects that attack our food crops. Among them are such chemicals as DDT, chlordane, and dieldrin—all of which are strongly suspected of being carcinogens. Likewise, the substances used in certain manufacturing processes—beryllium, chromium, and arsenic—are recognized as cancer-causing agents.

Perhaps the most widely feared of all the toxic pollutants are the radioactive materials and substances that are generated during—and then left over from—the production of nuclear energy. Some are highly radioactive, and some to a lesser extent. Some are liquids, while others are solids. They range from the assemblies that contain the atomic fuels used in nuclear production to the tools handled by workers. Their radioactivity has the ability to damage—even destroy—all life forms and the environment if allowed to escape into the atmosphere.

Because of their potential for harm, they must be kept safely locked away from the atmosphere throughout the production of the energy at nuclear plants. Unending care must be taken to prevent accidents and equipment failures that would set their radioactivity loose. Then, once they have been used and have become what are called nuclear wastes, they must be stored away from the atmosphere, in some cases for periods of up to 10,000 years or more before their radioactivity decays to the point where it is no longer dangerous.

Just what damage can radioactivity do to our bodies if it is released into the atmosphere? It can burn, trigger skin and internal cancers, and cause birth defects. It can result in radiation poisoning—an illness that, often fatal, strikes the central nervous system and causes diarrhea, nausea, chills, and the loss of the white corpuscles in the bloodstream. White corpuscles help the body fend off illness and disease.

As for the environment, radioactivity can sicken and kill plants and animals and leave broad stretches around the site of a nuclear mishap uninhabitable for years to come.

Two examples—one from wartime and the other from peacetime—can show us exactly how much harm radioactivity can do when set free in the atmosphere. In the closing days of World War II, the U.S. Air Force dropped atomic bombs on the Japanese cities of Hiroshima and Nagasaki. Each city was torn apart by a massive explosion. The two explosions took the lives of some 210,000 Japanese people and left thousands of others sickened and burned for life.

The worst atomic disaster in peacetime struck the nuclear power plant at Chernobyl in the Soviet Union. In 1986, an explosion shook the installation and hurled tons of radioactive debris skyward. The winds caught the debris and carried it out over a vast area. Some 2,500 square miles of land around the plant was rendered uninhabitable. Plants and animals in regions as faraway as Sweden, Norway, Great Britain, Italy, and Turkey were contaminated with radioactivity and could not be eaten safely. In the years since the catastrophe, an increasing number of cancer cases and birth defects have been reported in the regions near the plant.

Despite its dangers, nuclear energy is being widely employed for beneficial purposes today. It has, for instance, found a place in a number of medical procedures. More than twenty-five nations are using it to provide electrical power for their homes and industries. It is considered a fine tool for the production of electrical energy. So long as its radioactivity is kept safely penned, it does not stain the air with pollutants as does the burning of the fossil fuels. And it is considered a far less expensive power source than the fossil fuels.

To make certain that the radioactivity does not escape, work is continually being done to improve nuclear plant construction, equipment, and safety standards. The nuclear nations are working, singly and together, on the development of safe methods for the long-term storage of the nuclear wastes. Today in the United States, the nuclear wastes are being stored at plant sites or at designated commercial and government-owned locations. The U.S. has chosen two remote spots for the long-term underground storage of the wastes with a high level of radioactivity. One is located in New Mexico, and the other in Nevada.

A burial facility has already been built on the New Mexico site; it is not, however, being filled with wastes at present because water is leaking into it from the surrounding earth and threatening to corrode the containers in which the wastes are placed for storage. The Nevada installation is currently in the planning stages; because of delays in its planning, it is not expected to be constructed and opened until sometime in the next century.

THE POLLUTANTS IN SMOG

Many of the poisons that we've discussed hang about in the air, staining it a dirty yellow-brown, and become a part of what is popularly called *smog*, a term that was coined more than forty years ago from the words *smoke* and *fog*. It is true that many of the pollutants are smudging the air when smog is present, but smog itself consists principally of a gas that is formed through a photochemical process. It takes shape when the nitrogen oxides and hydrocarbons in the atmosphere react to the sunlight on a warm day and turn themselves into ozone.

Ozone, as you'll recall from Chapter 1, is looked on as a gas that is both helpful and dangerous. It is helpful in the stratosphere, where it shields us from the damaging ultraviolet radiation emitted by the sun. Here on earth, when formed by the chemical reactions of nitrogen oxide and the hydrocarbons to sunlight, it becomes a dangerous enemy. Scientists blame ozone for the heavy damage done to the vegetation in areas plagued by smog. As an example, they point to the hard-hit Los Angeles region. There, ozone is accused of damaging the area's citrus and grape crops and lowering their annual yields. And, in the nearby San Bernardino National Forest, it is charged with stunting the trees and causing them to lose their leaves.

Ozone is a bluish oxygen gas whose molecules contain three atoms rather than the two contained in ordinary oxygen atoms. The ozone that lies in the stratosphere is usually born of electrical storms at the equator and then distributed aloft by the winds. Ozone is also born in the stratosphere by the action of the sun's ultraviolet radiation on oxygen. Down here on earth, the gas can be created in laboratories by subjecting oxygen to a high-voltage electrical charge. It is commercially manufactured for such tasks as bleaching, sterilizing water, and removing unpleasant odors from foods. Ozone itself has a clean, pungent odor. We can often detect its odor in the air after a burst of lightning.

Smog, of course, is most prevalent in heavily populated areas that are highly industrialized and whose people depend primarily on the automobile for transportation. The cities afflicted by smog are located in all parts of the world. Included among those hardest hit are Tokyo, Japan; Mexico City, Mexico; Beijing, China; Essen, West Germany; and, in the United States, Los Angeles, Chicago, and Detroit. The problem, however, is not limited to major metropolitan areas. It is also found in small cities where there is industrial activity and heavy use of the automobile.

The contribution of the automobile, with its carbon monoxide, hydrocarbon, and nitrogen emissions, cannot ever be underestimated. It is considered to be the major cause of the smog endured by many cities, among them Los Angeles, which has the reputation of having the most polluted air in the nation.

Most seriously affected are areas where the winds are usually not strong enough to blow the poisons away—or areas where the geographical contours make it difficult for the winds to do their job. A prime case in point on both counts is the Los Angeles area.

The region lies in a basin that faces the Pacific Ocean on the west and is ringed by hills to the north, south, and east. The prevailing winds come from out of the Pacific and, often being little more than soft ocean breezes, are unable to lift the pollution across the inland hills. On occasion, however, the winds shift and, blowing hard, approach from the east. They sweep the pollution out over the Pacific, with newcomers to the area then being startled to learn what long-time residents have always known—that the Los Angeles air can be so crystalline that faraway objects seem to draw amazingly close. The region did not experience any smog problems until its population grew—and the number of its automobiles multiplied—during World War II and the years that followed.

A particularly annoying—and dangerous—ally to smog

is a condition known variously as a thermal inversion or a temperature inversion. To understand how it works, we have to begin with the fact that, under ordinary atmospheric conditions, warm air at ground level rises, becoming cooler as it travels upward. Pollutants are carried along on the upward rise and then can be better dispersed in the atmosphere. A thermal inversion, which often arrives in hot weather, sees a layer of warm air settle in over an area. It is warmer than the air below it and thus keeps the lower air—and the pollution in it—from rising. Trapped as it is, the lower air becomes increasingly filthy as more and more pollutants are added from car exhaust systems and industrial burnings.

The elements in smog, especially ozone, can induce a wide variety of physical discomforts. Stinging and watery eyes are commonplace, as are coughing, sneezing, choking, nausea, and shortness of breath. Of more serious consequence, there can be such troubles as heart problems and pulmonary edema, a filling of the lungs with fluid. Respiratory conditions, such as emphysema and bronchitis, can be worsened.

And, as you'll recall from the story of the 1952 London smog in Chapter 1, there can be death. The London tragedy, with its ultimate death toll of 12,000, ranks as the worst pollution incident on record. But it is far from being alone in the taking of life. Some sixty people died when Belgium's Meuse Valley was hit by a vicious pollution attack in 1930. Another attack, this one at Donora, Pennsylvania, in 1948, snuffed out twenty lives. In 1966, when a dense smog covered New York City for three days at Thanksgiving time, 168 people died. In all these instances, thermal inversions—or conditions similar to them—caused the air pollution to rise to deadly levels.

A thermal inversion occurs when a layer of warm air settles over an area and prevents the cooler air below it from rising. The lower air and the pollution in it are pressed back down toward the earth. It becomes increasingly filthy as the passing hours see it more and more filled with the pollutants from industrial burnings and car exhaust systems.

3

THE OZONE LAYER
Holes in the Sky

In 1985, alarming news reached the outside world from a British scientific team that had been studying atmospheric conditions in Antarctica for a quarter of a century. The team reported that a giant hole had been appearing annually in the ozone layer above the frozen continent since 1979.

The hole took shape at the beginning of each Antarctic spring (around mid-August) and remained in place for several weeks, usually closing up again sometime in October or November. Its size differed from year to year. In 1985, it was as large as the United States. It extended some 29,000 feet up through the layer, a distance equal to the height of Mount Everest, the tallest mountain in the world.

Why was the news from Antarctica so disturbing? To answer this question, we need to know what the ozone layer is and what it does for all living things here on earth.

THE OZONE LAYER

For billions of years now, the sun has bathed the world in light. It is a light that we all cherish and enjoy, but, as bright and cheerful as it can be on a spring day, it is an awesome force that holds many health dangers for us and our planet. They lurk in the ultraviolet (UV) radiation that emanates from sunlight. If we humans absorb too much of that radiation, we leave ourselves open to a variety of ills. If our planet absorbs too much of the radiation, all life here can be threatened.

Fortunately, nature provides us with a shield against the full force of UV radiation. Out in the stratosphere—at a distance ranging from ten to thirty miles above the earth—lies the ozone layer, the veil of gases that is named for its ozone content. Ozone, you'll recall, is made up of molecules that contain three atoms rather than the two found in ordinary oxygen. Though a dangerous element in smog here on earth, it serves as a protective shield out in space for a reason that is both simple and astonishing. Its molecules have the ability to absorb most of the ultraviolet radiation pouring into the layer. They allow only a small fraction of it to filter through and reach the earth.

Much of the ozone in the stratosphere is born during electrical storms near the equator, after which the winds shift it toward the polar regions. Rising all the while, it at last enters the stratosphere. Once there, it spreads itself in a veil over the world and proves to be the only atmospheric gas capable of blocking the flow of UV radiation. Just small amounts of it manage to do this vital job. Even where ozone gathers in its greatest amounts within the layer, there are only a few parts of it per million parts of other substances. Were you to transport all the ozone in the layer down to sea level and compress it, you would end up with a bluish sheet no more than one-tenth of an inch thick.

The full extent of ozone's value to us can be seen in one fact: the fraction of ultraviolet radiation that does manage to slip through the layer can do great harm when we are overexposed to it. It causes painful sunburns. Worse, scientists have linked it to various skin cancers and such eye problems as cataracts and damaged retinas. Further, there is evidence that it can weaken the immune system (the system that enables the body to resist sickness and infection) and render humans and animals more susceptible to illness.

Still further, scientists believe that the radiation packs enough punch to damage DNA (deoxyribonucleic acid), the chemical that is found in every living thing. If so, the radiation has the power to upset the workings of the cells in all life forms. This means that a prolonged and heavy radiation attack on DNA could lead to stunted and dying plant and animal life, with the result that the food supply would be drastically reduced in a world where there is already too much starvation. (Many physicians think that damage done to DNA by the radiation is the cause of certain skin cancers.)

The hole in the Antarctic sky indicated that we were losing some of the gas that is so precious to us. If the loss continued through the coming years—if the hole grew and spread its way across the world or if other holes began appearing elsewhere—we were due to be bombarded with greater and greater amounts of ultraviolet radiation, amounts that would no longer be just dangerous but deadly.

WHY THE ANTARCTIC HOLE?

The meteorological instruments used by the British scientific team revealed that the Antarctic hole (some scientists called it a "gap" or a "window") was not completely devoid of ozone. Rather, the amounts of the gas had dropped by varying degrees in different areas of the opening. Overall, the average amount of ozone known to be above Antarctica was down 40 percent in 1985.

Scientists quickly set out to learn what was causing the yearly opening. An international team traveled to the Antarctic in 1986 and was followed by a second group of 150 scientists from four nations in 1987. Flying into the stratosphere, both teams measured the ozone content and recorded the surrounding atmospheric conditions. Measurements and recordings were also made with instruments on the ground or hovering aloft in balloons. All this work showed that the hole was growing larger each year. In 1987, it was twice the size of the United States and speared its way up through the layer for a distance greater than the height of Mount Everest. Its ozone content was down 50 percent. In some areas, the gas had vanished altogether.

During the 1986 and 1987 investigations, scientists held several theories as to the cause of the hole. Some believed that brutal weather conditions above Antarctica were responsible for it. Others felt that some sort of solar activity might be to blame. And many suspected that a collection of gases manufactured down here on earth was at fault.

Originally developed by chemists in the late 1920s, these gases are made up of three substances—chlorine, fluorine, and carbon. They are known as chlorofluorocarbons

(CFCs). In the decades since coming into being, they have been used in an increasing number of commercial products throughout the world.

The work done in 1986 and 1987 cast a heavy suspicion on the CFCs. Weather conditions and solar activity were still thought to play significant roles in the Antarctic problem, but the two teams uncovered a strange fact that indicated the CFCs might be the true villains. The team measurements revealed the presence of heavy amounts of chlorine in the hole. The measurements also revealed that where the ozone content was most depleted, the chlorine was detected in its greatest amounts.

And there was another indication that the chlorine was at fault—one that could be seen in a simple laboratory experiment. When ozone was pumped into a tube and then joined by chlorine, the ozone immediately began to vanish.

Since the CFCs were heavily laced with chlorine and since the hole had appeared after they had come into worldwide use, it seemed obvious to many scientists that the gases were behind the problem. Escaping from the products in which they were used, they had made their way up into the stratosphere and were somehow tearing the ozone layer apart.

Though the idea that the CFCs were doing the damage seemed a good one, it was no more than a theory during the 1986 and 1987 investigations. Very soon, however, it was to prove itself correct. Today, science knows how the chlorofluorocarbons go about their destructive work in the layer.

THE CFCs: HOW THEY DESTROY

When the chlorofluorocarbons were developed by chemists at General Motors in 1928, they were looked on as "miracle" gases that could be safely used for many purposes. They were not toxic. They were not carcinogens. They did not corrode the materials with which they came in contact. Nor were they flammable. Finally, they could be manufactured easily and inexpensively.

In the years since their development, they have indeed been made to serve many purposes. Today, they act as coolants in refrigerators, freezers, home and automobile air conditioners, and factory and office cooling systems. In one of their most popular uses, they provide the jet streams that release the contents of aerosol spray cans—paints, shaving creams, deodorants, and such. One of their newest jobs is to clean the components in electronic circuitry.

The CFCs also go into the polystyrene material that is used in the manufacture of fast-food cups, dishes, and wrappings. By creating the bubbles that give this material its foamlike structure, they make it an ideal insulator against heat and cold. It keeps hamburgers, hot dogs, and coffee hot, while at the same time preventing ice-cold sodas from growing warm. These insulation abilities are now seeing the CFCs widely employed in the walls of homes and commercial buildings.

Over the years, the CFCs have been released into the atmosphere in great amounts. They are set free every time someone presses the button atop a spray can. They are loosed during their manufacture. And, though they are securely locked in refrigerators and similar products, they do manage to escape on occasion, most often in cases of accident or equipment leakage or malfunction.

But how do they go about their deadly work on entering the ozone layer? The answer begins with the fact that they are stable gases, meaning that they do not break up quickly on being released into the atmosphere at ground level. They are able to remain intact for years, sometimes for as long as a century. They spend several years—often about five—floating up to the stratosphere and into the layer.

Once they enter the layer, everything changes. They are hit by the full force of the sun's ultraviolet radiation and lose their stability. The radiation breaks them down into their three individual substances. The fluorine and carbon then seemingly do no harm. But not the chlorine. On being freed from its companion substances, it reacts chemically with the surrounding ozone and literally eats up the ozone molecules. Scientists have found that the chlorine does not attack the ozone just once. It reacts chemically again and again. These continuing reactions make it possible for a single atom of CFC chlorine to destroy as many as 100,000 molecules of ozone.

Accounting for the August appearance of the Antarctic hole is the fact that, beginning in March, the bottom of the world is cloaked in winter darkness for several months. Spring comes to Antarctica in August and brings the return of the sun and its intense ultraviolet radiation.

Scientists believe that, during the winter darkness, the CFCs and the ozone molecules attach themselves to clouds of stratospheric ice crystals. If this is actually the case, the chlorine is able to go about its destructive work with blinding speed when the returning sun breaks up the CFCs. The ozone molecules are clustered all around and locked in place on the cloud surfaces. The chlorine can devour them more quickly than would be possible if they were floating free.

It is known that other ozone-destroying gases have long been in the layer. These gases are generated here on earth and then mount skyward; among them is one that was mentioned in Chapter 1—methane. Because new ozone, after being born of electrical storms, was always arriving to offset the damage done by these gases, no real harm had ever been done to the layer. But now the CFCs have joined the other gases and have upset the balance of nature miles above our heads.

AN EARLY WARNING

Actually, the theory that the CFCs are damaging the ozone layer was not born during the 1986 and 1987 Antarctic investigations. It dates back to the early 1970s. It was a time when the gases were being increasingly employed because they seemed so safe to use. But 1974 brought the first ominous word that they might not be so safe after all.

The word came from two southern California chemists—Dr. F. Sherwood Rowland and Dr. Mario J. Molina. They announced that the CFCs were damaging the entire ozone layer. Two years earlier, they had learned that meteorological instruments were detecting traces of the gases in various areas of the layer. Since then, they had conducted a study of the stratosphere and the CFCs. It had led them to the theory that the gases were depleting the layer's supply of ozone worldwide and that the depletion would soon lead to an increase in the number of skin cancers.

Scientists gave the Rowland-Molina theory a mixed reception. Many felt that the two chemists were onto something. But just as many others disagreed with the idea and argued that, if there actually was an ozone loss, it was probably due to weather conditions or some sort of solar activity. Doubts about the theory, however, all but vanished in early 1988 when a group of more than 100 scientists from ten countries announced the results of a just-completed study.

The scientists had been assembled by America's National Aeronautics and Space Administration and had worked together as the NASA Ozone Trends Panel. For sixteen months, they had reviewed all available data on the condition of the ozone layer. The data, which included meteorological reports from around the globe, had shown them that the entire layer—and not just the section above Antarctica—was being depleted. They placed the blame directly on the chlorine in the CFCs. What they had to say was widely accepted as fact and the Rowland-Molina theory was acknowledged to be correct.

One aspect of the Antarctic hole had always been of some comfort to scientists. It was located above an uninhabited region. There was no human population beneath it to be harmed by the increase in ultraviolet radiation. But now, with the NASA Panel announcing that the layer was being shredded worldwide, harm seemed sure to come to large numbers of people.

Prior to the Panel report, many scientists had been worried that the Antarctic hole might one day pose a danger to humans living in the southern hemisphere. Their concern stemmed from two fears. First, the hole was annually growing larger and spreading closer and closer to the people of Australia and New Zealand. Second, there was the worry that, when it began to close each year, it sucked in the ozone from nearby inhabited areas—among them not only Australia and New Zealand but also the southernmost nations of South America—and left them vulnerable to increased UV radiation.

The worries about Australia were given substance in late 1987 when three out of five meteorological stations there reported a drop in the ozone content above the nation. The drop was most severe above the city of Melbourne, where it persisted for three long weeks.

A few weeks before the Panel's report made headlines, bad news came from the top of the world. In early 1988, a hole was reported above the Arctic Circle, an area that is populated by a relatively large number of people, among them Eskimos, Canadians, Icelanders, Scandinavians, and Russians. If the hole kept reappearing and growing larger, there could be widespread health damage.

All the bad news was capped off by the NASA Panel's report. The NASA scientists announced that the ozone loss was indeed global and that, worldwide, the layer's ozone content had fallen by 3 percent between 1969 and 1986. They then had this somber warning for everyone: if the loss continued at its present rate, the world was due to receive a highly dangerous 5 to 20 percent more ultraviolet radiation than usual in the next forty years. Making matters even worse was the fact that ultraviolet radiation is measured in wavelengths and that the most biologically damaging of their number are those known as UV-B. Most of the increased radiation expected in the next forty years will be of the UV-B type.

Thus far, we have briefly mentioned the harms done by UV radiation. Now, just how great will those harms be to Americans if we allow the increased radiation to go on attacking us through the coming years?

THE ATTACK: OUR HEALTH

The U.S. Environmental Protection Agency (EPA) is the federal office charged with safeguarding all aspects of our nation's environment. Using computers, it has made projections of the health damage that lies ahead if the attack of ultraviolet radiation is not turned back. The EPA admits that these projections may not prove to be entirely accurate over the years. But they do give us some idea of what an ozone-starved future threatens. Here are just three examples of what we may have to suffer:

> An additional 550,000 to 2.8 million cataract cases are expected to strike Americans born before the year 2075. Cataracts, which divide themselves into a number of different types, can be described as a film that forms on the lens of the eye and blurs the vision. Usually, they can be surgically removed with little difficulty, but if left untreated, they often lead to blindness; they are, in fact, one of the chief causes of blindness worldwide. Though able to strike at any time in life, cataracts are usually associated with old age. The EPA projections warn that, with the increase in UV radiation, they will begin to afflict younger people. If the prediction is correct, this means they will be harder to treat.

■

(The year 2075 is used as a benchmark in these projections because of the rate at which the concentration of the chlorine in the CFCs is growing in the stratosphere. Since the 1960s, that concentration has risen from 0.6 parts to 2.6 parts per billion other atmospheric substances. By

2075, even with the best of countermeasures, they are expected to be triple what they are today.)

It is estimated that every 1 percent drop in ozone will bring a 4-to-6 percent increase in such skin cancers as squamous and basal cell carcinoma. Should the ozone loss continue at its present rate, between 3 million and 15 million new cases of these cancers are expected to occur in Americans born before 2075. Squamous and basal cell carcinoma are two of the most common skin cancers and do not usually end in death. Nevertheless, the Environmental Protection Agency currently estimates that between 530,000 and a quarter million of the new victims will eventually die from these cancers.

■

The EPA projections indicate that an additional 31,000 to 126,000 cases of melanoma skin cancer will occur among Americans born prior to 2075. Melanoma is an extremely serious condition and is responsible for about 65 percent of skin cancer deaths. At present, some 26,000 new cases are reported in the United States annually. They result in approximately 8,000 deaths. The projected future increase in cases could lead to between 7,000 and 30,000 extra fatalities.

■

The people most vulnerable to skin cancer are Caucasians, particularly those with blue eyes and very light-colored skins. Many physicians worry that the people near or under the Antarctic and Arctic holes will be among the first to witness a major upswing in the number of skin cancer cases.

Intensifying this worry is the fact that the melanoma rate has already risen in a number of countries. It increased 87 percent in the United States during a seven-year period in the 1980s and is rising at a 3-to-7 percent rate in several other nations. In Australia, it is five times what it was fifty years ago.

Adding still further to the medical worry is the fear that the increasing UV radiation will weaken the immune system, the mechanism that enables the body to muster its own natural resources to resist illness and disease. If this fear is valid, we will be less able to fend off infectious disease and the development of tumors. In especially great danger here are people whose immune systems are already overtaxed in dealing with such diseases as AIDS and herpes.

Should the immune system be weakened, the inoculations that today safeguard us from such illnesses as tuberculosis and diphtheria will stand a good chance of becoming useless. When we are inoculated, we receive a small amount of the germs responsible for a given disease. We then suffer a very mild attack of that disease and ward it off with the help of the immune system. Though the attack can be so mild that we are unaware of its presence, we nevertheless suffer the disease itself and, as a result, are made safe from any future onslaughts. But suppose the immune system is no longer strong enough to work as it should. We might well develop the disease in its full-blown form—with possibly fatal results.

THE ATTACK: OUR WORLD'S FOOD SUPPLY

Research is leaving little doubt that the increasing radiation threatens to damage the world's food supply. A plant specialist, Professor Alan Taramura of the University of Maryland, pointed out this fact when being interviewed during a 1987 program on the ozone layer that was presented by the American Broadcasting Company's "Nightline" television news series. He said that researchers have studied more than 200 plant species and have found that about two-thirds of their number are prone to damage by increased amounts of UV radiation. He warned that some of the affected crops could disappear in time. Among them are such widely used foods as cucumbers, melons, cabbages, peas, and beans.

Today's research further indicates that the increased radiation will eventually damage photosynthesis in a plant. Photosynthesis is the natural process that, triggered by sunlight, makes it possible for a plant to form life-giving carbohydrates from the water and carbon dioxide in its tissues. Additionally, the increased radiation may hinder the plant's ability to take in and use water.

The overall result of this problem may well be a growing hunger worldwide as smaller and fewer plants become available for harvesting. A recent study by Professor Taramura revealed that a 25 percent loss in ozone reduced the yield of one type of soybean by as much as 25 percent. Soybeans rank high among the world's most important food staples.

Plants are not alone in being damaged. There is fear that sea creatures such as phyloplankton and zooplankton are already being sickened—and killed—by the increased radiation. These tiny beings are especially susceptible to harm because they live on the surface of the ocean and are constantly exposed to the sun's radiation. They are prime foods for the surrounding marine life. Should their number dwindle, the fish around them will begin to starve. In turn, the fish that survive long enough to be caught and marketed will be smaller and less nutritious than they are today.

A specific example of the harm that the increased radiation can do to the food supply is to be seen in a recent study of shellfish. It was found that in some species of shellfish a 10 percent decrease in ozone can lead to an 18 percent increase in the number of deformed or abnormal shellfish larvae.

Much worry is centered on the fact that the world's fish population is being severely decreased at present through overfishing for commercial purposes. Many marine biologists are concerned that the radiation damage will speed up the decrease by making it all the more difficult for the remaining fish to reproduce themselves.

On all counts, there is the specter of global food shortages and hunger if ultraviolet radiation increases.

4

ACID RAIN
"Death from the Sky"

In the 1970s, the press began telling us of a new environmental hazard. Reporters and commentators gave it a grim name, "acid rain," and described it in even grimmer terms as "death from the sky." It was, they said, falling on two adjoining regions—southeastern Canada and a broad expanse of the eastern United States. It contained acids that were poisoning some 50,000 lakes in the two areas and had already killed much of the life in their waters.

Since then we have learned much about acid rain. We know that it is now found in other U.S. areas and in such widely separated locales as western Europe and Mexico. We know that it stands accused of having the power to damage forests and vital food crops as well as freshwater fish. And we know it has the corrosive power to eat into and destroy the fabrics of the clothes we wear and the surfaces of the buildings in which we work and live.

Finally, we have come to know that the world's industrial nations, with their electric power plants and factories and automobiles, are in great part to blame for this "death from the sky."

WHAT IS ACID RAIN?

There are acids in all rain. Some are put there by nature and some are man-made. The term *acid rain* is the popular name for rain laden with a greater acidic content than normal. The term also applies to all other forms of precipitation—snow, sleet, hail, and fog—with an abnormally high acid content. *Precipitation* is the term for any moisture that comes from the atmosphere.

(Because the acids are found in the different types of precipitation, many scientists regard the term *acid rain* as being neither adequate nor accurate. They have replaced it with *acid deposition* or *acid precipitation*, each of which better indicates that the acids are deposited on earth by more than one atmospheric vehicle.)

Acid rain is caused principally by the industrial and automotive burning of the fossil fuels—coal, oil, and natural gas. When they are burned, they emit sulfur dioxide and nitrogen oxides. On rising into the atmosphere and being exposed to sunlight and moisture, the two substances undergo a chemical change. They dissolve into solutions of sulfuric and nitric acid, which then mingle with the clouds and return to earth in rain and its fellow precipitations.

As is true of other substances, the acid content in acid rain can be found by measuring the amount of hydrogen in it. (The hydrogen in acids is the cause of acidity.) The amount is measured on what is called a pH scale; the term *pH* refers to the number of hydrogen ions present in a liter of a substance. The scale extends along a range that counts from 14 down to 0. When measuring any substance for its acidity, one point must be kept in mind: the lower its count on the pH scale, the higher its acid content. For example, normal rain water has a pH count slightly over 5.6, while coffee comes in at 5.0, wine at 3.5, lemon juice at 2.0, and battery acid at 1.0. Pure water falls exactly midway along the scale—at 7.0. From the midway point upward, the scale measures substances containing increasing amounts of alkali, such as lye, which has a count of 14 and is extremely alkaline.

Scientists define acid rain as rain with a pH count of less than the 5.6 recorded by normal rain. They estimate that, when the pH count in acid rain stands below 5.0, the water into which it falls becomes so acidic that fish begin to die.

The difference in acidity between natural rain's 5.6 count and the dangerous 5.0 is great. This is because the pH scale is logarithmic, meaning that the acid content does not rise in single steps as the scale descends from, say, 6.0 to 5.0. Rather, the content rises in multiples of ten with each drop. Thus, a substance with a 5.0 count contains an acid content ten times greater than one posting 6.0. A substance with a 4.0 count is 100 times as acidic as a 6.0 substance.

WHERE ACID RAIN IS FALLING

Once we understand the way the scale works, we can get a good idea of the "bite" in the acid rain that has been falling on the regions most seriously troubled by the prob-

42 ■ OUR POISONED SKY

The pH scale is used to measure the degree of acidity or alkalinity in substances. The degree of acidity is counted downward from the point midway on the scale—from 7.0, which is the pH count for pure water. The lower a substance is found on the scale, the higher is its acid content. The degree of alkalinity is measured upward from the midway point on the scale.

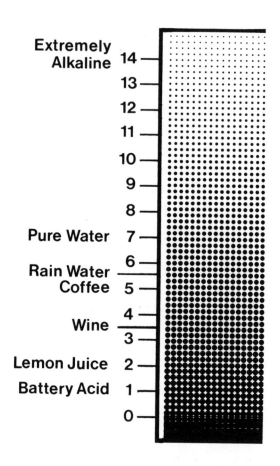

lem. The annual rainfall in broad areas of the eastern United States, southeastern Canada, and western Europe have pH counts ranging from 4.5 to 4.0. At 4.5, the acid content is more than ten times that of normal rain. At 4.0, it is ten times greater than the 5.0 at which fish are thought to begin dying.

The Environmental Protection Agency has developed statistics on the pH counts in the United States. As shown on the accompanying map, they are at their worst in a broad region of the nation's East, much of which has a 4.4 count. The area takes shape at the lower edge of Lake Michigan. It spreads to the Atlantic seaboard and fans out to the south and north—south to such states as Kentucky and Virginia, and north to the New England states (except Maine) and into southeastern Canada. An especially bad spot lies within the 4.4 zone. Blanketing parts of Ohio, Pennsylvania, and New York, it registers a 4.2 count.

Girdling the 4.4 region on three sides is a belt where the count stands at 4.6. It covers Maine and areas of southeastern Canada, sweeps down through Wisconsin and Illinois, and spreads across the south, running through such states as Tennessee, Alabama, and the Carolinas. Finally, there is a band with a 4.8 count. It spears out of Canada, runs through sections of the Midwest, and extends across the southernmost states from Texas to Florida.

Beyond these areas, except for a number of spots of heavy industrial activity, the United States enjoys a rainfall above a 5.0 count.

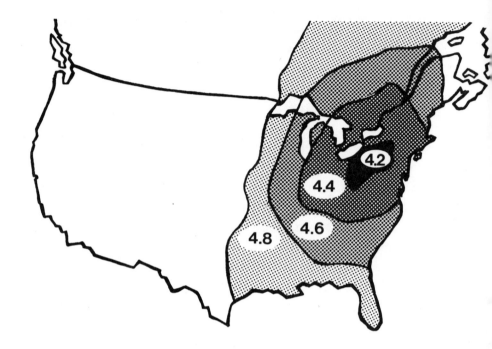

This map shows where the heaviest concentrations of acid rain are to be found in the United States. The acid rain problem is at its worst in a section of the nation's East, where the pH count extends from 4.2 to 4.4.

THE VILLAINS

Acid rain is usually seen in or near industrialized and highly populated areas. In the United States, most of the blame for the problem can be traced to the many coal-burning electric utility plants that are found in the Midwest and the East. Their smokestacks account for the major share of the sulfur dioxide that is emitted annually in the nation—some 67 percent. Industrial burning accounts for about another 11 percent. Other emissions—from car exhausts and the such—round out the picture with a contribution of around 22 percent.

As for annual nitrogen oxide emissions in the U.S., the electric power plants are running in second place. They are responsible for about 33 percent of all the emissions. Slightly in the lead are the nation's cars, trucks, and buses. They spew out some 38 percent of the total. Bringing up the rear are industrial burnings (about 13 percent) and other burnings (approximately 16 percent).

Greatly to blame for the fact that acid rain strikes the hardest in the eastern United States is the nation's basic wind pattern. Most of the country lies within the latitudinal band (30 degrees to 60 degrees North Latitude) where the prevailing wind comes from the west. The wind picks up

Much to blame for the severity of the acid rain problem in the eastern United States are the prevailing westerly winds in our country that pick up pollutants from industrial smokestacks in the Midwest, blow them eastward, and then fan them out along a broad north-to-south pattern.

much of the sulfur and nitrogen emitted in the Midwest, carries it eastward to mingle with the emissions already there, and then fans the entire lot out in a broad north-to-south pattern. Similarly, the 4.6 Midwestern band, though it loses some of its emissions, must suffer those that are carried in from the 4.8 band.

Though the winds may come from other directions in other parts of the world, the same pattern is to be seen wherever there is heavy acid rain. The regions that are hardest hit always lie in the path of the winds approaching from industrial and highly populated locales.

THE CANADIAN-AMERICAN TENSION

The acid rain problem is causing tension between the United States and Canada. Canadian scientists are accusing the U.S. of being responsible for much—if not most—of the acid rain that falls in their country. They contend that half the Canadian acid rain stems from U.S. emissions. They go on to claim that 75 percent of the rain in one area north of Toronto is the result of American emissions.

The Canadian claims may be correct because the emissions produced in the states adjoining eastern Canada are known to be three times greater than those generated on the opposite side of the border. Canada, however, recognizes that its own power plants and copper and nickel smelting factories produce their fair share of emissions. Ever since 1985, it has been embarked on a program to reduce the amounts of sulfur loosed from its smokestacks. In great part, the program is based on cutting back on the production that generates the sulfur emissions.

Canada is currently pressuring the United States to enact

legislation that will require the American utility industry to reduce its annual sulfur output. Canada wants to see the emissions reduced to half their 1980s level by the mid-1990s. The pressure is particularly strong because many Canadians feel that since their country is striving to cut its emissions, the United States should cooperate and do the same thing.

But representatives of the U.S. utility industry see the pressure as unfair. They contend that, to achieve the reduction sought by Canada, they would have to install expensive pollution-control equipment, such as scrubbers, which are devices that remove the sulfur from smoke. They argue that these additions would increase the price their customers have to pay for electricity and say that Canada is not installing the same kind of equipment. Rather, it is mainly cutting back on emission-generating production, something that the electrical needs of the U.S. make difficult to do.

Canada is countering the U.S. arguments with two principal replies: First, equipment to reduce sulfur emissions has been installed in four of its six major smelting operations; the six are responsible for 60 percent of the nation's sulfur emissions. Second, the country's utility power plants, which account for 16 percent of the sulfur emissions, have cut back on their production or have begun using coal with a lower sulfur content.

The U.S. utility representatives argue that the coal mines located closest to the nation's power plants all contain coal with a high sulfur content. The costs of transporting the high-sulfur coal to the power plants are low. Low-sulfur deposits are also available, but at a greater distance, meaning increased transportation costs that would raise the price that American consumers must pay for electricity.

The argument continues back and forth across the border.

THE ACID RAIN PUZZLE

Over the years, acid rain has been accused of doing many harms. But accusations are one thing, and *proof* of harm is another. Scientists have yet to establish beyond a doubt just how much damage the rain has actually done. In trying to do so, they are faced with a puzzle that consists of three major questions—questions that are easy to ask but difficult to answer.

1. Is acid rain completely to blame for the harms of which it stands accused—harms to freshwater life, forests, food crops, buildings, and even our physical health?

2. Or is it only partly to blame, with other forces, both natural and man-made, also playing major roles in triggering the damages?

3. Or is it completely innocent in some cases?

Scientific opinion is divided on the possible answers to these questions. Most scientists do not believe the rain is solely at fault for all the damage being done. Nor do most think it completely innocent of some harms. Rather, they feel that much of the havoc attributed to acid rain is actually the result of a combination of forces, some of which—such as the weather—are fashioned by nature, while others are the pollutants of our making. Acid rain has simply joined these forces to worsen matters.

An example of what is meant here was seen in 1989. Archaeologists reported that acid rain born of the smoke from factories in southeastern Mexico was eating into the nearby ruins of the ancient Mayan civilization, chipping away the stucco and flaking the paint on buildings, temples, and statues. That the rain is at fault can be clearly seen on the outer walls of one palatial building. Its west wall has been scarred over with black acid deposits, while the east wall has been left almost unmarked. The archaeologists said, however, that acid rain is not solely responsible for the damage. The weather must also take a share of the blame. The local winds consistently drive the area rains against the western side of the structure with a greater force than against the opposite side. Further, it is known that the weather has been eating away at the Mayan structures ever since they were built more than 1,200 years ago. Acid rain is simply accelerating the erosion process.

This example is an easily understood one. Things become far more complex when scientists attempt to gauge *exactly* how much blame can be placed on acid rain when it joins all the possible combinations of natural and manmade forces in doing harm. Now the questions of how guilty or innocent it actually is in certain cases become all the more difficult to answer.

Some possible answers have come to light as the result of present-day research. For one, research is showing that, at least to date, acid rain is not proving itself dangerous to our health. We can only hope that studies in the future will be able to reach the same conclusion.

But other of the answers are making the puzzle even more complex. This is because they sharply conflict with each other. As we'll now see, they have triggered a dispute among scientists over which are to be believed.

Lakes and Streams

As some researchers see things, there is little doubt that acid rain is mainly—and perhaps solely—at fault for the loss of much freshwater life. They point out that the pH count in a number of lakes and streams in Sweden, Norway, southeastern Canada, and the Adirondack Mountains of New York State has plunged to 5.0 and below since the coming of acid rain. The result: their fish populations have totally disappeared. (A pH count of 5.0, remember, marks the acidic level at which fish are thought to begin dying.)

Strengthening their view is a recent Canadian experiment. To assess the damage that acid rain might do, researchers deliberately increased the acid content in a lake relatively untouched by the rain. The experiment destroyed the crustaceans living on the lake bottom and stopped the fish from reproducing.

Other researchers, however, claim to have found evidence that acid rain may play only a small role—or none at all—in much of the damage. One research team recently studied some 2,800 lakes devoid of fish in the Adirondack Mountains. The team reported that in only 10 percent of the lakes could it blame acid rain for the absence of fish life.

The team members contended that, while acid rain certainly poses a danger to fish in areas of high sulfur emissions, it cannot be blamed for the acidity in every "fishless" lake. They said it has been mistakenly accused of killing the fish in many lakes that have had a high acid content throughout their histories and were without fish long before acid rain ever came along. Such lakes may never have had fish populations.

They went on to explain that the acid content in a freshwater body, whether lake or stream, depends on a variety of natural and man-made factors. Included in their number are: the chemistry of the water; the types of vegetation found growing on the bottom; and the acidity in the soils and fertilizers that flow into the water. The researchers felt that, as in the case of the Mayan ruins, it is a matter of acid rain adding to the work done by other forces and thus worsening matters.

For example, they said, suppose that a lake or stream with a high aluminum content in the sediment at its bottom is hit by acid rain. The increased acidity will leach out—free—the aluminum. The aluminum then becomes responsible for the harm that ensues.

The research team also noted that acid rain's ability to kill seems to depend much on the nature of a given lake. Harm may be done to one lake but not to another. Take, for instance, a lake that has always enjoyed a low acid content. It may well prove "sensitive" to the rain, meaning that its fish will die because they have never had the chance to build a natural resistance to the newcomer. It is in lakes such as these that the researchers think acid rain is mainly—if not solely—guilty for the damages done.

On the other hand, the team reported, some lakes seem to have the strength to resist harm. Their waters are blessed with a chemical makeup that is able to neutralize the increasing acidity. Further, some lakes boast fish that are impervious to acidity. One such species—the largemouth bass—has long done well for itself in Florida lakes with a seemingly deadly pH count of 4.5 to 4.0.

The research team belongs to a U.S. government task force known as the National Acid Precipitation Assessment

Program (NAPAP). Formed by Congress, it is charged with studying acid rain, assessing its damage, and then making recommendations for cleaning up the problem. NAPAP's membership consists of representatives from twelve government agencies, four national research laboratories, and more than 400 American and Canadian scientists. The task force began its work in 1980 and is scheduled to publish a final report on its study in the early 1990s. However, it issued an interim report in 1988. The team's lake findings were contained in the interim report.

But the report ran into trouble. It was sharply criticized by a number of scientists because it contained only the one lake study and not others that had been conducted at the same time. The critics charged that it had been limited to larger lakes only and thus produced misleading information. It should have also cited the results of studies made of smaller lakes—those under 10 acres in size—where the increasing acidity would be more quickly felt. Then the true extent of acid rain's treachery could have been better gauged. The critics said that from 10 to 19 percent of the smaller Adirondack lakes are showing a pH count at or below the dangerous 5.0 level.

Forest Damage

Research at North Carolina's Mount Mitchell, the highest peak in the eastern United States, provides evidence of the harm acid rain can do to forests. A prolonged study of trees at sixteen sites on the mountain has shown that their trees have suffered defoliation and an increasing death rate in recent years. The death rate rose from below 10 percent in 1984 to around 40 percent in 1987. Mount

Mitchell has long endured highly polluted air. At times, the pH count there has plunged to 2.6, meaning that the rain has about the same acid content as vinegar.

Similar studies have been conducted in the forests of West Germany, where the acid in the rainfall at times has been twice that recorded in the United States. These studies have tentatively placed the blame for slower-than-normal tree growth, lost foliage, and a rising death rate on acid rain.

The NAPAP interim report, however, says that other factors may be the major contributors to the forest damage. Among them are disease, drought, fire, insect attacks, and chemical changes in the surrounding soil.

Thought to top the list of all the culprits is ozone, which ranks as such a danger when it takes shape in smog. The report blames ozone for the heavy forest damage that has been seen over the years in the smoggy Los Angeles area. This view, which is widely shared by California scientists, has prompted NAPAP to think that ozone rather than acid rain might be the major culprit in areas located near other smog-troubled cities.

According to the interim report, it is possible that ozone is also much responsible for the harm being noted in eastern U.S. forests, among them the woods on Mount Mitchell. The ozone levels in these forests have been higher than expected in recent years. Said to be in particular danger are trees standing at loftier altitudes. It has been found that the ozone levels at higher elevations do not decrease at night as they do closer to sea level.

In addition, the NAPAP report points to the damage sustained by European forests in recent years. Scientists in Europe once thought acid rain to be at fault, but the report says they now believe the major causes of the damage to be ozone and the droughts suffered in 1975, 1976, 1982, and 1983. The long march of dry, sunny days generated an increase in the amount of ozone in the atmosphere.

Crop Damage

No other NAPAP finding has triggered more dispute than the one concerning the possible connection between acid rain and crop damage. In its interim report, NAPAP announced that its researchers have subjected some thirteen varieties of eight basic commercial crops—among them corn and wheat—to a simulated acid rain with a dangerous 3.8-to-5.0 pH count. The researchers said that the crops suffered no measurable and consistent damage to their yields.

The researchers felt that since American farmers manage their soils with irrigation and fertilizers, the acid rain would likely have little effect on crop production. They added that, in fact, the sulfur and nitrogen in the rain might be of benefit to soils deficient in these substances.

But, as was the case with other of its findings, NAPAP was accused here of reaching conclusions based on inadequate research. The critics said that it had researched just one-third of the nation's crops and had not included such basic foods as apples and peaches in its study. Consequently, no decisions on crop damage could be made until a wider study was undertaken and completed.

Further, the interim report was condemned as inadequate because no one can yet say whether NAPAP's simulated acid rain affects plantings in the same way as "natural" acid rain. The critics said that other studies have shown that acid rain with a lower pH count—3.0—than the simulated rain has damaged certain crop yields.

THE PUZZLE TODAY

And so, where do we stand today on the road to solving the acid rain puzzle? The NAPAP findings suggest that the rain may not be the awful villain that most people have thought it to be. But, though time may prove NAPAP correct, it should be remembered that the group's findings are general ones and are being seriously disputed by environmentalists. They cannot yet be accepted as solid truths. Much work remains to be done before the puzzle is finally solved and we all learn the actual truth of the matter. In the meantime, we have no choice but to consider the rain a major environmental and potentially catastrophic danger that must be faced and overcome.

5

THE GREENHOUSE EFFECT
A Dangerous Heat

In recent years, scientists have been warning us of the catastrophic harm that can be done to the world by the atmospheric warming known as the *greenhouse effect.* One such warning came from an environmental scientist during a 1988 program that the ABC television news series "Nightline" presented on the greenhouse effect. He said that the effect could bring record droughts, record heat waves, record smog levels, and an increasing number of forest fires.

Another caution comes from author Bill McKibben in his book, *The End of Nature,* which was published in 1989. He warns that the increasing atmospheric heat could melt the world's icecaps and glaciers, causing ocean levels to rise to the point where some low-lying island countries would disappear, while the coastlines of other nations would be drastically altered for ages—or perhaps for all time—to come. Today's major port cities would be inundated and rendered useless.

THE GREENHOUSE EFFECT

But just what is this feared and potentially devastating phenomenon known as the greenhouse effect?

The answer begins with the most basic of all the facts in the natural sciences: most of the earth's heat is provided by the sun. The sun radiates its heat in visible and ultraviolet (invisible) rays. When they reach us, the earth absorbs some of their heat and reradiates the remainder back into the atmosphere. The reradiated heat tends to work its way into outer space. Some of it manages to do so, but a major portion does not and, instead, is stopped by the gases and water vapor that make up the atmosphere. They serve as a barrier that first absorbs the heat and then reflects it down to earth. As a result, the earth receives an "extra share" of warmth.

This "extra share" provides us with much comfort. Scientists estimate that, without it, the earth would be from 18 degrees Fahrenheit to 32 degrees F. colder than is the case.

When traveling from the sun, the rays encounter the same barrier as the outgoing rays. Though it catches some and deflects them back out into space, it does not bother those of the ultraviolet type. They are "invisible" to the barrier and are thus able to slip through it undetected. But the same cannot be said of the outgoing rays. No longer ultraviolet in nature, they are "seen" by the barrier, stopped, and turned about for a trip back to the earth.

The term "greenhouse effect" came into use some years

The "greenhouse effect" is caused by gases and water vapors that are present high in the atmosphere. When the earth reradiates the sun's heat, these gases and vapors absorb the heat and reflect it back down to earth, making it comfortable for us. The problem today is that pollutants being spewed into the air are adding to the gases in the atmosphere and upsetting the balance. The increase threatens a dangerous rise in global temperatures.

ago because the barrier, when reflecting the heat back to earth, seems to be functioning in the same manner as the glass roof of a garden greenhouse. The glass roof allows the sun's heat to enter the greenhouse and then prevents the air that it warms there from escaping back out into the open.

Scientists point out, however, that it is technically inaccurate to compare the atmospheric heating to a garden greenhouse. They explain that much of the heating in the garden greenhouse is due to preventing outside air from entering the structure to mingle with and cool the inside air. Nevertheless, the term continues to be popularly applied to the heating now taking place in the atmosphere.

The greenhouse effect has been with us ever since the gases and water vapor that make up the atmosphere took shape eons ago. Then why is it considered such a danger today?

The answer contains two parts. First, the earth's climate has always undergone periodic changes, sometimes warming and sometimes cooling. Science knows, for example, that major cooling trends have been occurring for more than 700 million years. They resulted in the great Ice Ages that covered vast expanses of the globe with icecaps and glaciers. The most recent of these Ice Ages struck some 115,000 years ago and remained on the scene until the earth's climate entered a warming period about 15,000 years ago and slowly began to melt much of the ice.

What is important to us at present is the fact that scientists have noted that our climate has been embarked on a new warming trend since the early 1800s. When charted on a graph, this new trend shows a series of ups-and-downs, but an unmistakable general movement upward. At the present time, the global climate is about 1 degree F. warmer than it was at the opening of the twentieth century.

The second part of the answer centers on four of the gases found in the atmosphere—carbon dioxide, methane, the chlorofluorocarbons, and nitrogen oxide. They all occur here on earth and are distributed aloft by the winds.

We have already talked at length about the CFCs and nitrogen oxide, and so let us concentrate here on carbon dioxide and methane.

Carbon dioxide is a colorless, odorless gas that, as its symbol—CO_2—indicates, is constructed of one carbon atom and two oxygen atoms. It is formed with our every breath; we inhale oxygen and exhale carbon dioxide as a waste product. It is also absorbed by plants. Major amounts of carbon dioxide are emitted into the air when the fossil fuels and trees are burned and when plant and animal bodies decompose. Commercially, CO_2 is used in such products as carbonated beverages, refrigerants, and fire extinguishers.

Methane, too, is a colorless, odorless gas. It emanates from animal wastes, rises from the vegetation, insects, and bacteria in swamps, rice paddies, and termite mounds. It is given off in plant and animal decomposition. It ranks as a principal constituent in natural gas and is produced in petroleum refining. Methane is widely used as a fuel and is employed in the manufacture of certain chemicals.

With the exception of the recently invented CFCs, these gases have been released into the atmosphere for eons by natural forces that range from plant decay to forest fires, and have not caused a problem. The trouble is that, once again, our industrialized world is upsetting the balance of nature in the sky. Our industrial burnings and other activities have added so much to the amounts of the gases already in the sky that they are beginning to act in a harmful way. The greenhouse effect looms as a threat today because the global warming trend that began in the early 1800s is being accelerated by our incessant loosing of the gases. All are strengthening the atmospheric barrier and helping to push more and more heat back toward the earth.

The situation is worsened by the fact that the increasing heat warms the oceans and causes them to emit greater amounts of water vapor through evaporation. The vapor adds to the strength of the barrier and helps to trap and reflect earthward even more heat.

Actually, many scientists argue that the four gases are doing more than simply contributing to the warming trend. They believe the gases are causing it. As they see things, it is more than a coincidence that the trend began at the very time when industrialization was spreading across the world.

If these gases continue to pour into the atmosphere at their present annual rates, scientists predict that we will experience a rise in global temperature of 3 to 9 degrees F. sometime by the years 2040 to 2050. If the prediction, which is based on computer projections, proves true, the earth will be warmer than it has been in the last 65 million years.

WHAT MAY LIE AHEAD

A temperature rise of 3 to 9 degrees F. may not seem to be much of an increase. But consider this: in 1990, a National Broadcasting Company television special, "The Infinite Journey: Crisis in the Atmosphere," made the point that the global temperature rose by 9 degrees F. at the end of the last great Ice Age approximately 15,000 years ago. Over the following 10,000 years, that 9-degree increase melted enough ice to cause the world's oceans to rise 250 feet. Sea water flooded in over the edges of our continents and islands and drastically altered the shape of their coastlines. And so the predictions of what a 3-to-10-foot ocean rise can bring in the next forty to fifty years are dire. Here is what scientists are saying could happen:

A melting of the world's icecaps and glaciers could raise sea levels between 1 and 3 feet in that time. The rising waters could devastate shallow coastal river lands, among them Egypt's Nile Delta. They could cover up to 20 percent of such nations as Bangladesh. Such low-lying island countries as the Maldive Islands in the Indian Ocean could disappear completely. The same could happen to the Netherlands, which lies below sea level and has always depended on a system of dikes to hold the ocean at arm's length. In the United States, the incoming waters could flood and render useless such major cities as New York; Los Angeles; Seattle, Washington; Miami, Florida; and Galveston, Texas.

■

The rising ocean waters would have a detrimental effect on our freshwater supply. Salt water is unable to push far inland along coastal rivers because of the resisting pressure their waters exert on it. The rising sea level would overcome that pressure. Salt water would move far up the rivers and begin to deplete the supply of freshwater that we and all agricultural crops require for nourishment. In a 1988 issue of the *San Francisco Chronicle,* historian Harold Gilliam reported that Roger Revelle, a former president of the American Association for the Advancement of Science, believes that a rise of just 4 degrees F. could severely damage California. It could cut the state's water supply by more than half. This would turn half of California, one of the nation's major agricultural centers, back into the desert it once was.

∎

The rising temperature would not affect the climates in all areas of the globe in exactly the same way. In some regions, the annual rainfall would decrease or disappear altogether, while it would increase in other areas. A loss of rainfall in today's major agricultural regions would bring on droughts that would see crop shortages and widespread, even worldwide, famine. And there would be mass population shifts as people sought out once-arid lands where the new rain patterns make crop growth possible.

∎

Entire species of plants and animals could be wiped out. Or there could be massive population shifts of animals to new regions as, like humans, they searched for food. One way or the other, the world's ecosystems as we know them today would be drastically altered.

∎

For many—if not all—scientists, the greatest worry here centers on the fact that these changes will occur so quickly. As was pointed out on NBC's "Crisis in the Atmosphere," the world has undergone massive climatic changes before, but has done so at a much slower pace. The slowness has allowed the planet and most of its ecosystems to adjust to the alterations. But now, rather than occurring over periods of thousands of years, the changes are due to arrive within a half century or so. There is the deep fear that we and our world will simply not have time to adjust to them and thus will be unable to handle them and successfully alter our ways of life.

THE GREENHOUSE GASES

Of the greenhouse gases, the one doing the most damage is carbon dioxide. Predictions hold that if it continues being poured into the air at its present rate, CO_2 will be responsible for about 50 percent of the greenhouse-effect warming by the year 2020. The CFCs may have to take the blame for as much as 25 percent of the problem; methane for about 15 percent; and nitrogen oxide for perhaps 10 percent.

Carbon Dioxide Emissions

Industrial and automotive burnings of the fossil fuels account for most of the growing amount of CO_2 in the atmosphere. The current widespread felling of trees runs a close second.

Absorbing and then holding great amounts of the gas in their trunks, trees are excellent storehouses for carbon dioxide. When they are cut, their value as storehouses for the CO_2 already in the air is lost; when they are burned, their carbon dioxide content is loosed into the atmosphere. At present, there is heavy timber cutting worldwide. One of the regions hardest hit is South America's Amazon Basin. Its rain forests are being steadily axed and burned to make way for settlement, agriculture, and recreational purposes. Estimates hold that as much as a fifth to a quarter of the Amazon trees have already fallen.

In 1988, Worldwatch Institute, an American organization dedicated to studying global environmental problems, estimated that deforestation has poured 90 billion to 180 billion tons of CO_2 into the air since 1960. In the same period, Worldwatch said, the atmosphere has taken in 150 billion to 190 billion tons from the industrial and automotive burnings of fossil fuels.

The U.S. Department of Energy estimates that, of this awesome tonnage, about 5 billion tons are emitted annually by the burning of fossil fuels. Eastern Europe and the Soviet Union lead the world in annual emissions, with 1.3 billion tons. The United States follows with 1.2 billion tons. China comes in with a half-billion tons. Western Europe is responsible for 784 million tons.

Worldwide, the CO_2 emissions are increasing at a rate of 3.6 percent a year. Recent scientific studies of the gases trapped in glacial ice have shown how much the concentration of carbon dioxide has grown since the Industrial Age took shape. Near the close of the 1800s, when industrialization was becoming worldwide, the concentration stood at a safe 275 parts per million (ppm) of other atmospheric substances. Today, after advancing steadily through the years, the concentration looms at around 352 ppm. If the fossil fuels continue to be burned as they are today, the concentration will be twice what it was near the close of the 1800s by the year 2050.

It is then, many scientists feel, that we can expect to feel the first truly harsh effects of the greenhouse effect. In the meantime, two factors will tend to slow the advance of approaching trouble. First, it will be slowed by the ability of the world's oceans to cool the atmosphere. Second, since 1970, there has been a dip in the upward course of the global warming trend; the longer that dip continues, the better off we will be.

Methane Emissions

At present, an estimated 425 million tons of methane are being released into the atmosphere. The amount of the gas in the atmosphere has been regularly measured for just ten years. The measurement shows that it has been growing by about 1.1 percent annually. The concentration of methane in the atmosphere stands at 1.65 ppm. This is double the concentration estimated to have been present before industrialization.

Scientists warn that, as the climate continues to grow warmer, the amounts of methane being emitted could increase—this because the heat will cause dying plant and animal life to decay more rapidly than is the case today.

CFC and Nitrogen Oxide Emissions

The CFCs are, of course, double villains. They are not only able to destroy the ozone layer but are also able to help trap heat in the atmosphere and direct it back to earth. At present, the CFCs in aerosol cans alone are being released into the atmosphere at the rate of around 224,000 tons a year.

The amount of nitrogen oxide—or, as it is also called, nitrous oxide—being sent into the atmosphere is increasing by 0.2 percent a year.

ARE WE FEELING THE GREENHOUSE EFFECT TODAY?

Though the full impact of the greenhouse effect is not expected for another fifty to sixty years, some scientists contend that we are already feeling the beginnings of its harsh touch. To substantiate this belief, they point to one of the hallmarks of a warming climate—an increasing number of droughts. Though it has plagued the world for eons, drought has struck more often than usual during the past two decades.

Beginning in 1968 and extending into the mid-1970s, Africa's Sahel region suffered a drought that led to a widespread famine. By 1973, the lack of food and water had killed more than 100,000 of the region's people and several million of its cattle. The Sahel lies at the southern edge of the Sahara Desert and extends across Africa from the Atlantic Ocean to the Indian Ocean. Located within its boundaries are six countries—Senegal, Mali, Niger, Chad, Sudan, and Ethiopia.

During the 1970s and early 1980s, extended droughts struck other areas of Africa. In all, twenty-four African nations were affected. By 1984, more than 150 million African people were threatened with starvation due to drought-induced famine.

Nor was Africa alone in being attacked. The 1970s and 1980s brought droughts to such widely separated nations as Australia and New Zealand, Bolivia, Great Britain, Italy, the Soviet Union, and the United States. Some of the hottest and driest years on record in the United States occurred during the 1980s.

Though many scientists regard these droughts as signs that the greenhouse effect is already at work, just as many others disagree. There is a strong belief that factors having nothing to do with the greenhouse effect may account for the severe dry periods. For one, there is the theory that some of the droughts were caused by sunspot activity.

Sunspots, as their name indicates, are dark blotches that

can be seen periodically on the face of the sun. It has been found that when they appear, the sun will usually be marked with them for about eleven years. During that time, they grow in number—with some dying out while others take their places—and then fade away. That eleven-year period is known as a sunspot cycle. Though droughts can strike in any year, solar observations have long shown that they often arrive about every twenty-two years. Some droughts within the past two decades occurred at the end of such a cycle.

There are also strong indications that two giant bands of water in the Pacific Ocean were at fault for three global droughts that struck during the 1980s—in 1983, 1987, and 1988—and may have been responsible for a number of earlier attacks. Both bands take shape periodically near the southern tip of South America.

One band is made up of extremely warm water and is called El Niño (meaning, in Spanish, "the boy"). The other, which is known as La Niña ("the girl"), consists of extremely cold water. Though both bands take shape in the Pacific, they do not appear together. Rather, one—El Niño—comes into being near South America and spreads westward across the ocean. Then it fades away and is replaced by La Niña, which also fans out over the sea. Each lasts approximately three to four years. Both are strongly suspected of being able to trigger atmospheric disturbances—such as major shifts in wind patterns—that can induce periods of extremely dry and hot weather at widely separated points throughout the world.

■

News reports of the possibility that the droughts of the past twenty or more years have been generated by the above factors have caused many people to believe that the greenhouse effect may not be as dangerous as it is said to be. In the minds of many—if not most—scientists, this is a risky and mistaken belief. They see the greenhouse effect as one of the major environmental threats looming over the world. Something must be done quickly about it and all the other dangers we are facing because of the poisoning of our sky.

But what?

6

FIGHTING POLLUTANTS
The Worldwide Effort

Thus far, the material on the four global atmospheric problems has been grim and frightening. The time has come to remember a point that was stressed in Chapter 1: the situation is far from hopeless. Steps can be taken to reverse the terrible course of events in the sky.

Many such steps are already being taken. Let's take a look at what is being done, worldwide and in the United States, to cleanse the sky of pollutants and their resulting smog, and to solve the problems of the ozone layer, acid rain, and the greenhouse effect.

THE BEGINNING

The worldwide effort against air pollution dates back to 1964, when an organization called the International Union of Air Pollution Associations was formed. Its membership consisted of environmental groups from nine countries—Argentina, Australia, France, Great Britain, Japan, Norway, Sweden, West Germany, and the United States. Their job was to make recommendations on how pollution could best be controlled. Each member nation could then, if it wished, put the recommendations into practice at home.

Other organizations and efforts took shape as global pollution worsened during the latter half of the 1960s. In 1972, the United Nations sponsored a conference in Sweden to study the problem and its dangers. The next years saw individual countries move against the poisoning of the sky. It was—and continues to be—a move directed at two targets.

The first is that specific polluter, the car engine, which is credited with being the single greatest cause of smog in the world's major cities. (When we speak of the car engine, we are referring to both the gasoline and diesel engine.) The second can be called general air pollution. It is made up of all the poisons that come from our industries, our homes, and our daily use of chemical products.

THE CAR ENGINE

Just what is being done to offset the harms done by the car engine? One answer comes from the automobile manufacturers in various countries, among them Great Britain, Japan, and the United States. Over the years, they have placed an increasing emphasis on lightweight cars that provide a greater fuel efficiency—namely, vehicles that give a greater number of miles per gallon (mpg) of gasoline. They have done so because a car that averages, say, 25 mpg obviously releases far fewer pollutants than one that averages 15 mpg. Unfortunately, as reported by *Time* magazine in 1989, many Americans, after turning to smaller cars during the fuel shortages of the 1970s, have begun using larger "gas-guzzling" models again.

Another answer comes from the petroleum companies that have cut the amount of lead additive in their gasolines. Sometimes doing so on their own and sometimes on orders from their governments, they have been producing gasolines with a low-lead content or none at all. This effort, which began in the early 1970s, has turned out to be a highly effective antipollution measure. In the United States alone, it has caused the lead particles emitted by car exhausts to drop by 90 percent.

Still another answer comes from Japan. Ever since the mid-1970s, Japan has required all cars, trucks, and buses to be fitted with equipment meant to reduce or eliminate the pollutants that escape from tailpipes. Japan's national and local governments routinely inspect vehicles to see that the equipment is functioning properly.

Actually, Japan is just one of many nations that require equipment to limit automobile fumes. Similar laws are on the books throughout the world—in, for example, Australia, Canada, South Korea, Sweden, Norway, Switzerland, and the United States. Unfortunately, however, some other countries have not followed suit. Little or nothing, for example, has yet been done about auto emissions in smog-ridden Argentina, Mexico, and India.

What kinds of equipment are being used to control car emissions in the nations with antipollution laws? Several types are available. One is a pump that forces air into the exhaust system; the additional air burns up the carbon monoxide and the hydrocarbons coming from the engine cylinders. Another is known as the exhaust gas recirculation (EGR) system; it returns some of the exhaust fumes to the engine. They lower the engine temperature. The drop in temperature then reduces the amounts of pollutants being formed.

The emission-control device that has found the greatest use worldwide is the catalytic converter. Developed in the U.S. during the 1970s, it is a tubular chamber through which the exhaust fumes must pass before escaping into the air. It contains pellets of heat-resistant materials coated with a mixture of metallic elements. The metallic elements most often employed are platinum and palladium. They catch the passing carbon monoxide and hydrocarbons and generate a chemical reaction that converts the former into carbon dioxide, and the latter into water vapor.

The device is called a catalytic converter because the

Used in automobiles to reduce dangerous exhausts, the catalytic converter contains pellets of heat-resistant materials coated with such metallic elements as platinum and palladium. As exhaust fumes pass through a chamber filled with the pellets, they catch the carbon monoxide and hydrocarbons and change them into carbon dioxide and water vapor. The dark area in the center of the drawing represents the chamber in which the pellets are stored.

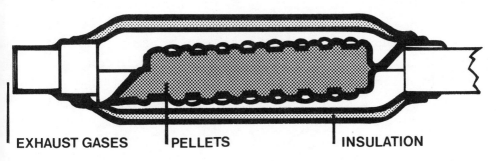

metallic elements serve as catalysts that trigger the chemical changes in the pollutants. Though the converter gets rid of two engine pollutants, it creates another problem in that it replaces the carbon monoxide with carbon dioxide, that major contributor to the greenhouse effect.

A number of countries are also working to reduce tailpipe emissions in other ways. Several have placed restrictions on the amount of driving that can be done in their most polluted cities; such restrictions are in force in Budapest, Hungary; Athens, Greece; and Rome, Italy. Research on the development of electrically powered cars is being pursued in Europe and the United States.

In the United States, work on an electric car is advancing beyond the research stage. In 1990, General Motors Corporation unveiled what it called a "full-performance" experimental electric car. Christening it the Impact, General Motors announced that the vehicle can reach a maximum speed of 75 miles per hour and travel up to 120 miles between battery charges. The company explained that the car, a teardrop-shaped two-seater, runs on two alternating current-type motors. They are powered by an 870-pound pack of conventional lead batteries. Each motor drives one of the front wheels. The car develops 114 horsepower. A General Motors spokesman said that the company might be able to mass-produce the Impact within four or five years.

A thorn in the side of manufacturers who wish to develop an electric car has always been the need to recharge its batteries, a job that takes about six hours to complete. In the spring of 1990, the city of Los Angeles and the Southern California Edison power company announced plans for a $2 million test project that will see electric cables placed under a 1,000-foot-long stretch of freeway in the western area of the city. Power from the cables will be used to run electric cars and to recharge their batteries when drivers plan to operate them on conventional roads. If the test proves successful, the future may see other Los Angeles roads electrified. However, city and power company officials warn that a widespread electrification of roads in Los Angeles and elsewhere remains in the distant future. Billions of dollars and long years of construction will be required before roadway electrification becomes commonplace.

In yet another effort to reduce tailpipe emissions, some nations are showing an increasing interest in the use of alternative fuels—fuels that contain either a low petroleum content or none at all. Heading the list of countries looking into these fuels are Brazil and the United States.

Ever since the early 1980s, Brazil has sponsored a program that encourages its motorists to use clean-burning sugarcane alcohol as a partial substitute for gasoline. The program was launched as much to help Brazil's economy as to cleanse its air. As one of the world's largest importers of cars and oil, the nation was facing an annual petroleum bill of over $10 billion. It decided that it must lower this yearly debt by using a home-grown product to meet some of its vehicular fuel needs. By the close of the decade, the alcohol derived from sugarcane was providing approximately half of Brazil's automotive fuel.

The U.S. Congress in 1988 enacted legislation that urges carmakers to mass produce two types of engine, each of which will be able to operate on fuel containing a mixture of gasoline and another substance. One type would use a mixture containing 85 percent ethanol or methanol (both are forms of alcohol). The other, called a fuel-flexible engine, would run on assorted blends of gasoline and alcohol, or on a combination of natural gas and gasoline.

The alcohol fuels are widely seen as being excellent future replacements for gasoline. But, as the Worldwatch Institute, the American organization that is dedicated to studying global environmental problems, comments in its book, *State of the World 1989,* they pose a number of problems.

For one, they are being currently tested to see how much they may actually improve the quality of the air. Thus far, the tests have produced mixed results. Much in question is the advisability of using methanol. On the one hand, some methanol blends have been found to give off hydrocarbons in very small amounts and so promise to help the smog problem by retarding the development of ozone. On the other hand, they do little to reduce carbon monoxide emissions. Conversely, certain other blends reduce monoxide emissions, but do nothing to cut back on the pollutants that lead to the creation of ozone.

Another problem: one source of methanol is coal. Coal, as you know, contains carbon, and so the methanol that comes from it emits carbon dioxide, as do the methanol products from other sources. If used in great quantity, it could add significantly to the greenhouse effect.

Finally, the other major alcohol type—ethanol—can be obtained from grain crops, among them corn. If manufactured in great quantities, it would cut deeply into the amounts of a crop that would be needed as food. Some 40 percent of the yearly U.S. corn crop would be required to provide enough ethanol to meet 10 percent of the country's automotive needs.

GENERAL POLLUTION

General air pollution—the poisoning caused by industrial smokestacks, home chimneys, and the manufacture and use of chemical products—is being attacked in various ways by different countries. Great Britain has struck at the problem with its Clean Air Act, which was prompted by the deadly London smog of 1952. Enacted into law in the 1960s, the measure gives local authorities the right to establish "smokeless zones" in highly polluted areas, meaning that the authorities can ban the use of such smoky fuels as coal and require the adoption of cleaner-burning substances. The Act has proved a great success. An example of its effectiveness was seen as early as 1970, when once smoggy London began to be applauded worldwide for its clean air.

Brazil, along with countries such as Japan and Australia, is seeking to reduce the danger in its industrial smoke by requiring factories to install equipment that will help their smokestacks prevent the escape of pollutants. High on the list of this equipment are the scrubbers that remove sulfur and other pollutants from smoke. Japan requires the use of such equipment in cities where weather conditions and the contours of the land trap the pollutants in the local air and keep them in place.

Several European nations are emphasizing the careful placement of new factories. The intent here is to locate the factories in spots where their smoke will do the least amount of damage to populated regions and recreational areas.

Though scrubbers are widely used, some of the world's

78 ■ OUR POISONED SKY

factories are also turning to other antipollution procedures. One of the most interesting is known as electrostatic precipitation. It removes solid particles or fluid mists from fumes with the aid of electricity. On entering a special chamber, the polluting substances are given a positive electrical charge, after which they flow past an area in the chamber where its surfaces carry an opposite—negative— charge. They are attracted to the surfaces and are then held there while the fumes, now free of contaminants, travel up a smokestack and into the outside atmosphere. Later, the chamber walls can be cleansed of the polluting substances.

Electrostatic precipitation is employed to cleanse factory smoke. The pollutants pass through a chamber where ionizers give them a positive electrical charge, after which they flow past surfaces that carry an opposite—negative—charge. They are attracted to the surfaces and held there while the smoke, now free of pollutants, escapes into the atmosphere.

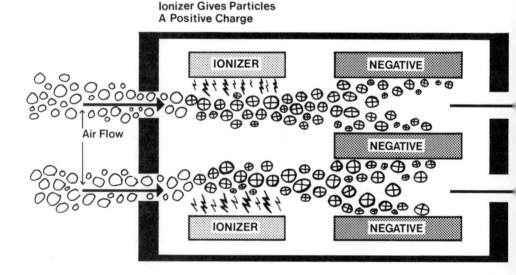

Fighting Pollutants: The Worldwide Effort ■ 79

Some antipollution procedures are primarily aimed at sulfur, which, along with causing acid rain, is a major health menace in itself. One is called fluidized-bed combustion. It requires that pulverized coal be burned in a bed of limestone or dolomite. The alkalines in these substances absorb the sulfur and turn it into an ash that can then be removed from the furnace.

One measure that has been tried in the United States and elsewhere has proved of questionable value. It calls for raising the height of industrial stacks so that their smoke can be better caught and carried away by the wind. The strategy has helped to clear the surrounding air, but has worsened matters in distant areas that lie in the path of the wind-borne pollutants.

Various nations are beginning to replace the burning of coal (and its fellow fossil fuels, oil and natural gas) with other power sources. In the main, these sources are intended to provide the countries with electricity. India wants to develop solar power facilities. More than twenty-five nations are now using nuclear energy. Despite the hazards involved in its production, they have turned to the energy for several reasons—partly because they see it as a major power supply for the future, partly because it produces electricity more cheaply than does the burning of the fossil fuels, and partly because, if its radioactivity is kept safely away from the environment, it does not pollute the air as does the burning of fossil fuels.

The nuclear countries are located on all continents and range in size from such small nations as Bahrain and Israel in the Middle East to such giants as Canada, China, the Soviet Union, and the United States. At present, nuclear energy is providing about 15 percent of the world's electrical power. The United States is the largest user of the energy. It maintains 114 nuclear power plants (as of 1989) in more than thirty states. They provide between 18 to 20 percent of the nation's electricity.

■

The antipollution efforts, worldwide and in the United States, have been many. But they prompt a question: How successful have they been—how much have they actually cleansed the air? We will look at some answers after we have seen in greater detail the American efforts being leveled against the car engine and general air pollution.

One of the worst episodes of heavy smog in the United States occurred at Donora, Pennsylvania, in 1948. It claimed the lives of twenty people. In this photograph, the pollution seems to be a thick fog as it obscures the city's streetlights at night. (AP/Wide World Photos)

RIGHT: *Los Angeles, California, ranks high among American cities hardest hit by air pollution. Here, smog is seen obscuring the buildings in the city's central area on a June morning in 1988. At the center is the Los Angeles City Hall.* (AP/Wide World Photos)

BELOW: *Air pollution in Washington, D.C., during the late 1970s caused a cyclist to wear a protective mask as he traveled to work.* (AP/Wide World Photos)

Pollution is such a problem in Los Angeles that electric signs are posted along the area freeways to warn when smog conditions are becoming extreme and to urge motorists to reduce the number of cars on the road by car-pooling. (AP/Wide World Photos)

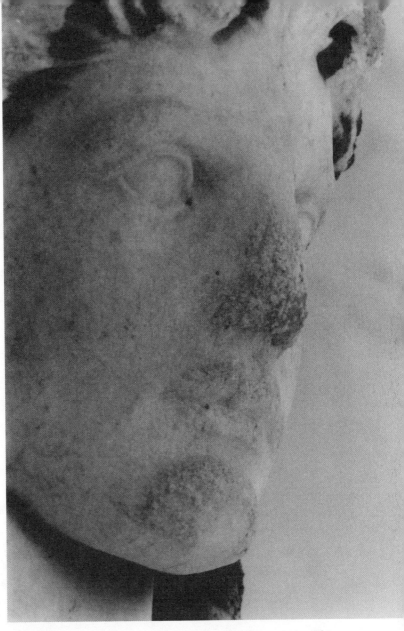

Officials at the Field Museum of Natural History in Chicago say that acid rain is responsible for the damage done to the nose and chin of this statue, which stands outside the museum. (AP/Wide World Photos)

ABOVE: *Unveiled in 1990 by General Motors, the Impact is an experimental electric automobile that may be ready for mass production within four or five years. Engineers at General Motors say that the car can attain a maximum speed of 75 miles per hour.* (Courtesy of General Motors)

BELOW: *The Impact is powered by an 870-pound pack of conventional lead batteries. According to General Motors, the car can travel up to 120 miles between battery charges.* (Courtesy of General Motors)

Heightened factory smokestacks reduce the pollution in the surrounding air. The increased height enables their smoke to be more easily caught and borne away. But while the atmosphere around factory sites is cleared, the winds carry the smoke to distant areas, where it has increased pollution problems and caused acid rain. (AP/Wide World Photos)

By steadily warming the earth's atmosphere, the increasing greenhouse effect is expected to cause serious consequences, among them a growing number of droughts. Here, a Kentucky farmer views the ruins of his soybean crop during the severe drought of 1988. (AP/Wide World Photos)

7

FIGHTING POLLUTANTS
The American Effort

In the United States, the campaign against the car engine (both the gasoline and diesel engine) and general air pollution is being carried out along three fronts—at the federal, state, and local levels.

THE FEDERAL LEVEL

The federal government's antipollution efforts began in the mid-1950s when Congress authorized a program to give financial and technical aid to state and local governments that were trying to combat the problem. At that time, as a result of the growth of our cities and industries during World War II, air pollution was well on its way to becoming the major environmental threat it is today.

The federal aid proved of little help. Air pollution continued to worsen. In 1963, Congress tried another financial measure, the Clean Air Act, which granted additional funds to state and local governments. When money again could not solve the problem, Congress broadened the scope of the Act in 1968 by adding legislation that called for car manufacturers to develop equipment to reduce carbon monoxide and hydrocarbon emissions. But, by 1970, the country's sky had become so poisoned that it was everywhere causing deep public concern. Congress responded to the concern by strongly amending the Act. The amended Act struck at pollution in three ways.

First, it set its sights on the nation's automobiles. The aim was to get rid of 90 percent of the carbon monoxide, hydrocarbons, and nitrogen that they emitted. In keeping with the 1968 legislation, carmakers were ordered to devise special emission-reduction gear for their engine systems. Now, however, they were given additional instructions: have equipment to end carbon monoxide and hydrocarbon emissions installed in all new cars by 1975—and equipment to stop the nitrogen emissions in all 1976 models.

Second, the amended Act required the federal government to establish standards of cleanliness for the nation's atmosphere. The standards were to set limits on the emission of some 300 pollutants by the nation's cars and industries. To help meet these standards, industries were given five and a half years to make significant reductions in their smokestack releases of such major pollutants as suspended particulate matter, sulfur, the hydrocarbons, and nitrogen.

Factories were left to decide how to achieve the cuts. They could, for instance, elect to install special equipment, such as scrubbers, or turn to the use of fuels containing fewer pollutants. The Act also outlined the penalties to be assessed when a manufacturer failed to make the necessary reductions. A first failure could bring a fine of $25,000 a day (until the problem was corrected) and a one-year prison term. A second failure could see the penalties doubled. Additionally, regions that failed to comply with the new standards could suffer the loss of federal funds to help pay for state highway construction. The funds would not be awarded until the regions brought their air up to snuff.

Finally, the amended Act authorized the federal government to establish a new office—the Environmental Protection Agency (EPA). Hitherto, a number of different federal agencies—such as the National Air Pollution Administration and the Federal Water Quality Administration—had attended to the country's various pollution problems. Now the EPA took over the responsibility of safeguarding all aspects of our environmental welfare. Today, it enforces federal regulations on matters that range from air and water pollution to the use of pesticides and the safe production of nuclear energy.

In early 1990, President George Bush elevated the head of the Environmental Protection Agency to a position on the President's Cabinet.

The federal standards for clean air were established soon after the amended Act was passed into law. Covering substances that range from suspended particulate matter to sulfur and ozone, they stipulate the maximum possible amounts in which each pollutant may be present in the atmosphere during a given period of time. For example:

Carbon monoxide: A maximum of 35 parts per million (ppm) of other atmospheric substances for one hour, or 9 ppm for eight hours.

Ozone: A maximum of 0.12 ppm for one hour.

Sulfur dioxide: A maximum of 0.14 ppm for 24 hours, with an annual mean not to surpass 0.03 ppm.

Nitrogen dioxide: An annual mean no greater than 0.05 ppm.

The EPA monitors the air quality at points throughout the nation. Over 5,000 stations have been established for the job.

STATE AND LOCAL LEVELS

A number of state and local governments have not depended solely on the federal Clean Air Act for controlling atmospheric pollution within their borders. They have enacted laws and programs of their own. Two cities did so before there was a federal Clean Air Act—Pittsburgh and Los Angeles. Their programs date back to the 1940s.

You'll recall from Chapter 1 that Pittsburgh, as one of the nation's chief industrial centers, was early plagued by the smoke from its factories, so much so that it passed its first smoke abatement laws in 1812. But 133 years later, the city was again in trouble. By 1945, its factories had so multiplied that their smoke was often turning day into night. At times, street and automobile lights had to be kept on throughout the daylight hours. The municipal government took action and passed strict antipollution laws. The result: daylight returned to Pittsburgh within a few years.

Los Angeles undertook a similar program in 1947. Once a place of clear skies, it was now suffering dirty air and smog. The city fathers blamed the growth of local industry during World War II for the problem. They passed a set of laws that required all businesses—from manufacturing plants to junkyards—to clean up their operations. The city's air began to clear.

But it cleared just a little. Any real gain in the air quality of Los Angeles itself and the surrounding area was offset by a steady and mysterious increase in smog. In 1950, a research study solved the mystery by demonstrating that the smog problem could be traced to the pollutants being spewed from the region's automobiles. The number of cars had been mounting as more and more people moved to southern California over the years. The people all depended on their cars to get about because the area did not—and still does not—boast a widespread public transportation system.

Nothing was done about the thickening smog throughout the 1950s, but the state legislature acted in the 1960s at the urging of Los Angeles officials. It adopted laws saying that, in the near future, all new cars had to be fitted with emission-control equipment before they could be sold in California. When the U.S. Congress in 1968 strengthened the federal Clean Air Act by calling for the development and use of automotive emission-control gear, it was following California's lead.

Today, California's antipollution laws are recognized as the broadest and strictest in the nation—stricter even than those imposed by the federal government. Service stations must use special nozzles to prevent the escape of fumes when gasoline is being pumped. Every car built since 1973 must contain emission-control devices before it can be sold in the state. (This requirement predates by two years the time set by the 1970 amended Clean Air Act for the placement of the controls in vehicles.) All cars, regardless of their age, must periodically undergo "smog control" tests at state-approved garages and service stations. The tests are meant not only to determine whether the emission controls are working properly but also to see that all older cars without the controls are not emitting too many pollutants. Cars that fail the test must be repaired immediately.

The California laws are not directed only at the automobile. They are also hard on industrial emissions. The state recently passed a law that requires future refiners to reduce the sulfur content to 0.05 percent from the average 0.25 percent previously allowed.

Another example: In 1986, the California legislature enacted a measure that attacked pollutants suspected of being toxic. It struck at them in two ways. First, it established a scientific process for determining whether any of a wide variety of air emissions are toxic. Second, it set up a procedure to be followed in controlling any emission found to be toxic. The measure then stipulated that all local districts are to follow the control procedure once an emission is identified as toxic. The measure opened the way to an extensive study of the possible toxicity of some 300 chemicals.

California was one of the first states to recognize the dangers posed by auto exhausts and general air pollution. It is acknowledged to be the nation's leader in fighting the atmospheric poisons, so much so that a number of states are considering the use of its laws to help solve their own pollution problems. Among them are New York, New Jersey, and all of the New England states. They believe that the use of the California laws would see the northeastern U.S. enjoy a significant drop in its automotive emissions by the year 2010—a drop of 39 percent in carbon monoxide emissions, 27 percent in nitrogen emissions, and 16 percent in hydrocarbon emissions.

Texas is also considering the adoption of the California laws. Other states are taking steps of their own. Colorado is planning to mandate the use of alcohol blends in its cars to help meet the federal air standards. New Jersey is imposing new environmental taxes. New Jersey, New York, and the New England states are uniting to work together on the pollution problems that plague their region.

SUCCESSES AND FAILURES

Worldwide and in the United States, the efforts leveled against the car engine and general air pollution have been many. But how much good have they done? How much have they actually cleansed the air? The answer is that they have yielded mixed results.

On the one hand, there have been major successes. For example, the mid-1980s saw ten nations score a triumph over the sulfur smoke that causes not only dangerous general pollution but acid rain. They were among twenty-one European countries that, in 1985, agreed to slice their sulfur emissions some 30 percent by 1993. Worldwatch Institute, in its book, *State of the World 1989*, reports that just one year later, in 1986, the ten had reached that goal. Four of their number then set out to achieve a 70 percent reduction.

Other successes: In 1989, *The New York Times* reported that the presence of lead in the U.S. atmosphere has fallen by 90 percent since 1970. Responsible for the drop is the fact that the use of lead additives in gasoline has been banned nationwide. Also in 1989, the Environmental Protection Agency announced a national ban on the use of asbestos, whose dust is known to be carcinogenic. The ban covers 94 percent of all products containing asbestos, including roofing materials, pipe wrapping, and automotive brake systems.

On the other hand, there have been failures. For one, Europe, in its attack on automotive exhausts, has thus far failed to exercise any significant control over the fumes emitted by the diesel engine. Physicians consider diesel fumes to be even more dangerous to health than those escaping from the gasoline engine. Worldwatch Institute reports that diesels are highly popular in Europe (as of 1986) and have captured some 18 percent of the new-car market there.

For the most part, however, the antipollution efforts have produced results in which both success and failure are mingled. During the 1970s, carbon monoxide emissions dropped by one-third in the United States and by 50 percent in Japan. But the drops in the two nations failed to improve in the 1980s. They came almost to a standstill and seemed ready to reverse themselves as more and more cars came into use over the years. *Time* magazine reported in 1989 that Americans now own more than 135 million automobiles, are driving more than ever before, and, after more than a decade of buying small fuel-efficient cars, are returning to bigger "gas-guzzling" models. Roughly one-third of all the world's cars are found in the United States.

There is also the fact that successes in some parts of the world have been offset by problems elsewhere. For example, while there has been improvement in the air quality of Great Britain and, as we shall see, the United States, the reverse is true in many Third World nations—in Africa,

Asia, and South America. These nations, where the price of a car was once beyond the reach of most people, are now witnessing a heavy increase in automotive use. Their air is steadily worsening because they have yet to adopt and enforce firm emission-control measures.

In the United States, there is widespread agreement that the amended Clean Air Act of 1970 has improved the quality of the nation's air over the past twenty years—but only to a limited extent. Statistics show that there have been modest reductions in the emissions of four of our major pollutants—carbon monoxide, sulfur, the hydrocarbons, and solid particles. There has been hardly any reduction at all in the emissions of another major poison—nitrogen.

Modest though the overall reductions may be, *The New York Times* in August, 1989, praised the amended Clean Air Act, saying that without it the country's air would likely be as choked with poisons as the highly polluted air of Mexico City. Earlier that year, *Time* said that the country has made "significant strides" in cleansing its atmosphere over the past years.

But, despite the good done by the amended Act, the nation's air remains dangerously dirty. Both Worldwatch Institute and the EPA recently drove this point home. Worldwatch reported that, in 1986, between 40 million and 75 million Americans were living in regions that failed to meet the federal clean-air standards. The Institute added that sixty-two American cities were failing to meet the federal standards for carbon monoxide and ozone.

The EPA upped both figures in a 1989 report. The agency announced that upwards of 100 million Americans live in polluted air and that more than 100 cities are failing to meet the nation's clean-air standards. The agency, however, contended that the quality of U.S. air was better than it was a decade ago.

Some states and cities are unable to bring their air up to federal standards through no fault of their own. This is because air pollution knows no boundaries. It is being carried to them from elsewhere on the winds. Connecticut Senator Joseph I. Lieberman recently remarked that even if his state were emptied and turned back into a wilderness, its air would still violate the federal standards because of wind-borne pollution.

And some cities are unable to control pollution because of their continuing growth. Despite California's strict laws, Los Angeles faces a constantly worsening air problem, so much so that the city is planning a new antipollution campaign in the 1990s. If it goes into effect, it will see tougher-than-ever laws against the manufacture of chemical products and especially against the automobile. Car pooling, alternative fuels, reduced car use, tighter emission-control regulations, and a call for increased use of public transportation are planned as mainstays of the campaign.

Opposition to the Act

In the main, the amended Clean Air Act of 1970 has done only a limited amount of good for three reasons.

First, as soon as it became law, the Act ran into trouble from the nation's car manufacturers. They complained that they could not develop the emission-control equipment demanded by the Act and have it ready in time to meet the 1975 and 1976 deadlines set by Congress. As a result of these complaints, Congress moved the deadline for the installation of the equipment back four times between 1970 and 1980.

Second, there has been continuing opposition to the Act from other quarters. Industries have argued that the costs of installing the smokestack equipment necessary to meet the federal clean-air standards are prohibitive and threaten their survival as businesses. Many of the nation's highly industrialized states agree and argue that the collapse of the industries within their borders could cost their people countless jobs. Environmentalists claim that the opposition to the amended Act has caused the EPA not to enforce the federal standards as strongly as possible.

Opponents of the Act have been accused of selfishly endangering the nation's health for their own economic good. They defend themselves by asking: "What good will it do to have the cleanest air in the world if everybody is out of work and going hungry?" They argue that a balance must be found that accommodates both the need for clean air and the need for all the industries and businesses that provide the nation with employment.

The industrial and state opposition prompted Congress to amend the Act again in 1977. Passed that year was a measure stipulating that no state may adopt its own clean-air regulations but must adhere to the federal standards. In the main, the measure was aimed at states that, to protect the industries and workers within their borders, might enact regulations that did not measure up to the federal standards. California was exempted from the measure because its standards and regulations often exceed federal standards and were in effect before the 1977 amendment was passed.

Finally, natural forces beyond our control—weather conditions—have hampered the progress that could be made under the 1970 Act. The 1980s were marked with drought years—times of dryness and harsh sunlight that contributed to the nation's smog problem. The EPA reported that the level of smog-inducing ozone increased 5 percent between 1986 and 1987. The level rose another 14 percent in 1989.

A New Clean Air Act

The condition of the U.S. atmosphere continues to be so dangerous that, in mid-1989, newly elected President George Bush proposed that the Clean Air Act be revised and strengthened. A committee of members of the House and Senate took up the matter, and finally reached agreement on stricter standards and new timetables. A bill presented to Congress won approval in October, 1990. Mr. Bush signed it into law.

The new Act sets stronger-than-ever regulations for the control and reduction of the nation's major pollutants and establishes dates by which the reductions are to be realized. Here are its major provisions:

Motor Vehicles: Tailpipe emissions of nitrogen oxides and hydrocarbons are to be cut by 35 percent and 60 percent respectively in many new cars starting in 1994 and in all cars by 1996. Oil companies are to develop and offer cleaner-burning gasolines, with 1992 set as the year for selling the cleaner fuels in cities suffering the worst carbon monoxide concentrations.

■

The Ozone Layer: The production of CFCs and carbon tetrachloride is to be phased out during the 1990s and is to be completely outlawed by January 1, 2000.

■

Urban Smog: Cities are to reduce their smog cover within a given period of time. Depending on the severity of a city's smog problem, the period may be as short as three years or (as in the case of extremely polluted Los Angeles) as long as twenty. Most cities are expected to make a 15 percent reduction in six years.

■

Acid Rain: The amount of sulfur dioxide and nitrogen oxide pouring from industrial smokestacks is to be sliced in half. Sulfur dioxide is to be cut to 10 million tons annually by the year 2000. Half that reduction is to be achieved by 1995, when the nation's 111 largest sulfur-emitting electric power plants in twenty-two states will be required to meet stricter emission standards by employing either sulfur-cleansing systems or coal with a lower sulfur content.

■

Toxic Pollutants: For the purpose of developing emission control standards, some 189 substances are to be listed as toxic air pollutants, and the EPA is to list 250 categories of pollutant releasers (oil refineries and chemical plants, etc.). The largest polluters are required to install grade-A emission-control equipment between 1995 and 2003. The aim is to reduce the emissions of toxic air pollutants as much as 90 percent by 2003.

■

Finally, the revised Clean Air Act calls for the establishment of a program that will provide compensation for workers who lose their jobs because of the new air standards. The program is estimated to cost about $250 million.

8

■ □ ■

WHAT ABOUT THE OTHER MAJOR PROBLEMS?

We turn now to the steps being taken against the three remaining worldwide problems caused by the poisoning of our sky: (1) the damage being done to the ozone layer, (2) the harms being done by acid rain and by (3) the greenhouse effect.

THE OZONE LAYER

You'll recall from Chapter 3 that, in 1974, when Drs. Rowland and Molina announced their theory that the chlorofluorocarbons were shredding the ozone layer, it was given a mixed reception by scientists. Many believed that the two California chemists were onto something, while just as many others disagreed with the idea and argued that any loss of ozone overhead was likely due to weather conditions or some sort of solar activity.

The reaction of the U.S. public, however, was anything but mixed. The idea that the CFCs were harming the layer angered and frightened countless Americans. Their concern was directed at what they saw as the most obvious cause of the problem—the CFCs that were being released daily from the millions of spray cans that gave us such products as hair sprays, shaving creams, deodorants, and paints. At the time, the cans were spitting 445,000 tons of CFCs into the atmosphere each year. Being released were the two CFC compounds that served as aerosol propellants—CFC-11 and CFC-12.

Heard everywhere was the demand that the federal government take action against the CFCs. In 1978, the government responded by banning their further use in aerosol cans and calling for the development of other, safer propellants. Joining the U.S. in the move were Canada, Norway, and Sweden, where the public fears were equally great. Together, the four nations reduced the use of CFC-11 and CFC-12 in 90 percent of their aerosol products.

The ban, of course, helped, but did not solve the problem. Other nations, especially those in Europe, continued to manufacture CFC-laden aerosol products. In 1980, however, a number of European nations decided not to increase their annual manufacture of aerosol CFCs but to hold it at the level achieved that year. They also announced that they planned a 30 percent reduction of the aerosol CFCs by 1982.

The four-nation ban and the actions then taken by the European countries led to a drop in the amount of aerosol CFCs being loosed yearly—a drop from the 445,000 tons of the mid-1970s to a present level of around 224,000 tons.

However, though CFC-11 and CFC-12 are also employed in other products, the aerosol cans are still ranked as the prime emitters of the two compounds. They use some 33 percent of all the CFC-11 and CFC-12 now being produced. The drop in aerosol emissions sounds hopeful until we check the amounts of CFC-11 and CFC-12 being released from other products. In 1985, the total CFC-11 emissions worldwide came to 238,000 tons. For CFC-12, the total stood at 412,000 tons.

The next step in the anti-CFC fight came in 1987. It was then that the representatives of twenty-four nations, deeply concerned over the giant hole in the ozone layer above Antarctica, met in Canada and developed the agreement known as the Montreal Protocol on Substances that Deplete the Ozone Layer. In the pact, the nations agreed to:

Freeze all CFC production at 1986 levels, with the freeze to take effect no later than 1989.

Achieve a 20 percent cut in global CFC production by 1993.

Cut production another 30 percent by 1998.

The nations also elected to freeze the production of another gas—halon—by 1992. As would be the case with the CFCs, the gas was to be frozen at its 1986 production level.

Halon serves worldwide as the propellant in fire extinguishers. It was developed by the U.S. Army late in World War II as a weapon for fighting blazes in armored vehicles and tanks. It was included in the Montreal Protocol because of its bromine content. Halon, like the CFCs, makes its way into the stratosphere where its bromine content is suspected of hastening ozone depletion by helping the chlorine in the CFCs to react with the ozone molecules.

In the years since the Canadian meeting, a number of other countries have joined the original twenty-four in signing the Protocol. The pact went into effect in 1989 and is presently signed by thirty-five nations, with perhaps more signatures to come in the near future.

As helpful as it is, the Protocol troubles many people. They want to see all CFC production banned immediately so that the stratosphere will be cleansed of the gases all the more quickly. They point out that the CFCs already in the atmosphere will take up to five years or so to reach the ozone layer and begin doing harm. Consequently, we are due to have an ozone problem for years to come—a problem that will continue to stretch out in front of us for as long as the CFCs are manufactured, even in the reduced amounts established by the pact.

There are several reasons why the pact calls for a step-by-step reduction in the use of the CFCs rather than an immediate outright ban. As is the case with the control measures for other pollutants, a principal one is economic. Many of the twenty-four nations balked at a complete ban because the CFC industry (which includes everything from the manufacture of the gases themselves to the manufacture and sale of the products in which they are employed) is a major one for them. An immediate and total ban would have cost them and all their people who work in the industry billions of dollars.

This may make it seem that the twenty-four nations are gambling with the world's well-being for the sake of their own economic interests. It should be remembered, however, that the pact also calls for the nations to review the status of the ozone layer in the early 1990s. On the basis of what they find, they then may decide on more stringent CFC curbs.

The Protocol countries also hope their projected CFC reductions will not be the only ones made. They hope that individual nations, cities, and industries will help by cutting the use of their own CFCs and by developing safer replacements. It is a hope that is being realized today in a number of governmental and industrial actions. They are actions that are being directed against not only the aerosol compounds but against all the other CFCs as well. For example:

Belgium, Great Britain, Holland, Switzerland, and West Germany have announced that they will cut back on all their various CFC uses some 90 percent in the 1990s.

Denmark has banned the use of spray cans employing CFC propellants. The ban was ordered in 1987.

The Soviet Union, one of the world's major users of aerosol cans, has stated that it will turn to non-CFC propellants by 1993.

A number of companies, in the U.S. and elsewhere, are employing systems to recycle the CFCs used as solvents to clean electronic circuitry. Recycling will keep a major share of the CFCs from entering the atmosphere. An International Business Machines plant in West Germany has installed a system that reclaims between 70 and 90 percent of its solvents.

ACID RAIN

Over the years since acid rain made its first appearance in the 1970s, many ideas have been proposed to cleanse it from the U.S. skies. Most have been aimed at reducing the sulfur being emitted by our factories and electric power plants; it accounts for some 65 percent of the acidity in the nation's acid rain. Congress has considered bills ordering that all coal-burning factories and power plants install scrubbers, those devices that remove most of the sulfur content in smoke. Other proposed congressional measures would allow the states to decide whether they wish to install scrubbers or turn to the use of coal with a lower sulfur content. Still other proposals have called for the country to slice its sulfur emissions—which now stand at 20 million tons a year—in half.

All these ideas have run into stiff opposition and have never been enacted into law. Again, as in the efforts to control other pollutants, economics lie at the core of the matter. Representatives of industry and electrical power plants complain that the measures could be put into practice only at great expense—an expense that would end up adding to the costs that consumers must pay for electrical service and a wide variety of manufactured products.

There is no doubt that the expense would be great. The Environmental Protection Agency recently estimated that it would cost between $16 billion and $33 billion over the next twenty years just to reduce the nation's annual sulfur emissions by half. A major part of this expense would involve a switch to coal with a lower sulfur content. As was mentioned earlier, most of the coal that lies near our industrial centers and electrical power plants contains a high degree of sulfur. Low-sulfur coal is to be found at greater distances and, consequently, would cost more to transport to the points where it is to be burned.

Another example of the opposition encountered by the proposals: congressional legislators from coal-producing states have opposed the cutback in emissions because it promises to take jobs away from the coal miners they represent.

But, despite the strong opposition, the country has managed to take several steps toward easing its acid rain problem. First, a number of factories and power plants have installed scrubbers on their own or on orders from their states. Some have turned to fluidized-bed combustion, the sulfur-reduction system that was described in Chapter 6. Other companies are using a method that entails the crushing of coal so that its sulfur content can be removed. The power industries in many states have abandoned coal and have turned to nuclear energy and hydroelectric power to generate electricity.

Also of help is the amended Clean Air Act of 1970. Sulfur ranks high among the pollutants affected by the nation's clean-air standards. The Environmental Protection Agency has established a regulation that requires all new coal-burning factories and electrical power plants to be equipped with scrubbers. Environmentalists, however, criticize the regulation as being of limited help because it applies *only* to new installations and ignores all those that have been spewing sulfur into the air for years. They feel that the Agency is bowing too much to the pressure exerted by the opponents of the anti-acid rain measures and, as a result, is gambling with the health of the people in the regions hardest hit by the problem.

THE GREENHOUSE EFFECT

At present, an extensive campaign against the greenhouse effect has yet to be launched by the world's nations together or by the United States alone. The current situation is this: the steps that are being taken to end other environmental problems also hold the promise of helping to slow—at least somewhat—the speed at which the globe is warming.

Take the CFCs as an example. They are expected to account for as much as 25 percent of the greenhouse effect by the year 2020. The Montreal Protocol, with its hope of safeguarding the ozone layer through cutting CFC emissions in the 1990s, will certainly be of some benefit in retarding the growth of the greenhouse effect. But, of course, this benefit will be of limited value, pertaining as it does to a substance responsible for only 25 percent of the trouble.

Or take the nitrogen oxides, which play a minor role in the greenhouse problem. A major step was taken against them in a 1989 pact signed by twenty-five nations, including the United States. The agreement calls for the countries to limit their nitrogen oxide emission levels to those prevailing in 1987. They are to do so beginning in 1994. The principal target here was the reduction of acid rain, but there was a simultaneous benefit for the retarding of the greenhouse effect. However, the benefit is of limited value because the oxides are expected to be responsible for only 10 percent of the greenhouse problem by 2020.

The major greenhouse gas, of course, is carbon dioxide, with predictions holding that it will account for 50 percent of the effect by 2020. The clean-air controls now being exerted on the burning of fossil fuels, especially coal and oil, by industries, electrical power plants, and automobiles will help cut the amounts of CO_2 entering the air—and, since nitrogen oxide is also emitted by factories and cars, they should aid in lowering its atmospheric count.

But, overall, the carbon dioxide picture is bleak. The heavy cutting and burning of many of the world's forests continues unabated, with the loss of every tree meaning the loss of a highly efficient CO_2 storehouse, and the burning of every tree—commercially or in an accidental forest fire—marking the release of more CO_2 into the atmosphere.

The burning of fossil fuels is accelerating with the growth of industry and the increasing number of automobiles worldwide, causing carbon emissions to rise by some 3.6 percent a year. That annual percentage may suddenly soar even higher: China has announced it is planning to double its burning of coal at the dawn of the new century as it attempts to better its economic position in the world through industrialization.

Especially troubling to Americans is the 1989 report of a study made by the World Resources Institute. The U.S., with its clean-air standards, had been thought to be making progress on curbing its CO_2 emissions, but the Institute study indicates that exactly the opposite is true. The Institute reported that the country's emissions rose more rapidly in 1988 than in 1987. In 1988, the U.S. emissions increased 4.1 percent, as compared with the global increase of 3.6 percent.

A Greenhouse Campaign Soon?

There is the widespread feeling that the industrialized nations of the world, the United States among them, have not yet mounted an extensive campaign against the greenhouse effect because they are reluctant to do so. If indeed there is a reluctance, there are at least two reasons for it.

First, many scientists question whether the problem is approaching as quickly as predicted and whether its consequences will be as disastrous as thought. They dispute the computer projections of a 3-to-9-degree rise in global temperature by 2040 to 2050, saying that the projections are prone to error and cannot cover all aspects of the future. They also point out that the projections sometimes disagree. In 1989, England's chief meteorological office reported that its latest projections indicated that the estimate of a 9-degree increase should be dropped by at least 5 degrees.

In all, these many scientists openly admit that they do not know exactly how much the world's temperature will rise in the next fifty to sixty years.

Second, there is a deep worry among the world's nations that an extensive campaign will prove so costly that many—perhaps most—countries will be able to undertake it without destroying themselves and their people economically. The estimated expense of limiting carbon emissions over the next century in the U.S. alone runs from a low of $800 billion to $3.6 trillion.

These costs, plus those of cleansing the sky of its other problems, would severely strain the budget of every American household—in taxes, in the rising cost of goods made scarce by a slowing of industrial production, and in jobs lost when certain factories go out of business or halt their operations while installing new anti-emission equipment or converting to alternative fuels. If the strain would be great in the U.S., can you imagine what it would be in less wealthy nations?

When the two reasons are joined, it becomes easy to understand the reluctance to launch an extensive campaign. With science uncertain of how much the greenhouse effect will actually heat the sky, no one can say what sort of campaign will be required.

Will we need an all-out effort, one that will not only drain the world economically but also turn the daily lives of its people upside-down in countless ways—in everything from the amount of money they earn and save to the ways they heat their homes, the products they buy, and the transportation methods they use? All these sacrifices will have to be made if we are indeed headed for a time of incessant droughts and the famine they threaten, and a time when rising ocean waters will drastically alter today's continental and island outlines.

Suppose the computer projections are inaccurate. Suppose that the heating will not be as great—or as fast in coming—as predicted. Then lesser measures could handle the problem. Would it then be wise to launch an all-out campaign? Might it not do as much harm as the greenhouse effect itself?

What is needed immediately is more study of the greenhouse effect; only by understanding what truly lies ahead can we determine the extent of the measures that will be needed to combat it. Some progress is already being made in this direction. The United Nations is sponsoring worldwide discussions of climatic conditions and is seeking to develop an international agreement on how to deal with changes in the climate. In the spring of 1990, the United

States sponsored an international conference on global warming. Representatives from eighteen countries attended the meeting. They heard President George Bush ask that their time together be spent in a debate on the scientific disagreement over the questions of how serious the greenhouse effect really is and how rapidly the world is actually warming. Most of the foreign representatives, however, felt that such a debate was unnecessary, saying that they believed the greenhouse effect to be a real danger in need of decisive counter measures. Mr. Bush replied to their concern by repeating a pledge that he had made soon after the start of his presidency—to have the U.S. cooperate fully with the United Nations in the effort to work out the international agreement for dealing with climatic changes.

When Mr. Bush requested a debate rather than calling for antiwarming action by the conference, he earned the criticism of many environmentalists. They have long held that he is not acting swiftly enough against global warming and other atmospheric problems. In the President's defense, however, it must be said that he has committed the United States to a broad study of all aspects of global warming and has earmarked $1 billion for the undertaking, which is to begin in 1991. Mr. Bush has also committed the U.S. to phasing out production of all CFCs as a means of easing both the problem of the greenhouse effect and the damage being done to the ozone layer; his plan calls for CFC production to end by the year 2000. Further, the President is calling for the nation to plant a billion trees to absorb CO_2 from the atmosphere.

9

WHAT YOU CAN DO TO HELP

Atmospheric pollution, worldwide and in the United States, is such a massive and complex problem that many people feel helpless to do anything about it as individuals. Actually, nothing could be further from the truth.

History is dotted with instances where just one person or a few people have successfully ended a danger or an injustice by speaking out and taking action against it. They were successful because their concern awakened the concerns of the people around them—and, in some cases, the concerns of people throughout the world. Each of us can be just as successful if we will only speak up and take action against the poisoning of our sky. In voice and action, each of us can communicate our concerns to others and inspire them to pass the message on to still others. Who knows how far the message will travel?

But what can each of us say and do? Here are ten ideas

that, beginning today, you can put to use as you work for the return of a clean sky.

1. Find out all that you can about air pollution. New facts about its spread and its dangers are constantly coming to light. Further, we can be certain that many new and ugly pollution problems will take shape during the coming years. And so we all have much to watch for and learn. Remember also that atmospheric pollution is just one of the environmental problems threatening us. Filth is also staining our lands and seas. Learn about what is happening to them, too. The more you know about all types of pollution, the better able you will be to act against them.

To help you on your way to finding out more about today's environmental problems, here is a list of some fine books on the subject:

State of the World 1989: A Worldwatch Institute Report on Progress Toward a Sustainable Society. Lester R. Brown, editor. W.W. Norton, 1989.

Design for a Livable Planet: How You Can Help Clean Up the Environment. Jon Naar. Harper & Row, 1990.

The End of Nature. Bill McKibben. Random House, 1989.

Saving the Earth: A Citizen's Guide to Environmental Action. Will Steger and Jon Bowermaster. Knopf, 1990.

Planet Earth. Paul Weiner. Bantam Books, 1986.

You'll also find much information in magazines and your local newspapers. Whenever you come across a particularly valuable article or news item, why not share it with your friends, mention it in class, or pin it up on your school bulletin board?

2. Many groups and organizations are dedicated to solving environmental problems. Found at the local, state, national, and international level, they keep track of dangerous polluting practices, inform the public of their dangers, and urge officials to control them. Among the best known groups are the Sierra Club, the National Wildlife Federation, and the Audubon Society. Join such a group. It will keep you abreast of what pollution is doing worldwide. And, by becoming part of such a group, you will be adding your voice to the demand for action.

3. Talk to your family and friends about atmospheric pollution. Try to alert them to the dangers that it holds for everyone. At school, why not gather some of your friends together and present a program on the problem for your class or for a school assembly? And why not form a school club that is dedicated to studying and discussing not only air pollution but all other types of pollution?

You can further help to make people aware of today's poisoning of the sky by participating in local, state, national, and international events that are dedicated to safeguarding the environment. An international event of great importance is the observance of Earth Day, which was held in 1970 and 1990. Participating in the 1990 observance were an estimated 200 million people in 140 countries.

When taking part in such events, however, be very careful of how you behave. Be sure that you do not litter the area and leave piles of trash behind. Many of the people who attended the 1990 Earth Day programs in such cities as Los Angeles, San Francisco, New York, and Chicago discarded tons of fast-food containers, soft-drink cans, plastic bags, and food scraps and dropped them on the ground for work crews to clear away. Along with the trash, they left the impression that they did not really care about the environment but were attending the Earth Day events because they thought them to be giant parties.

4. Support all national, state, and local efforts to reduce and even eliminate dangerous automobile emissions. Drive a car that is fuel-efficient; have nothing to do with models that are gas-guzzlers. Support the adoption of alternative automotive fuels. Reduce your amount of driving as much as possible; rather than hopping in your car, ride a bicycle or walk to school, the library, or the corner grocery store. If you must drive to work or school, form a car pool. Learn to use public transportation. If your area is without an adequate public transportation system, support actions in favor of installing such a system or expanding and improving the present one.

5. Study and encourage the use of alternative energy sources for industry, the production of electricity, and the heating of homes. Chief among these sources are solar energy and nuclear power. Insist that nuclear energy, should it come to your area, be safely and carefully used.

6. Speak out against the widespread destruction of the world's forests. Urge that, whenever and wherever a tree is cut down, another is planted to take its place. At home, help to store carbon dioxide away from the atmosphere by planting trees and bushes in your backyard. You can also join a local group that is dedicated to planting trees and bushes on parkways and along the streets. Encourage your school to sponsor a tree-planting program on each

Arbor Day—and then take an active role in making the program a success.

7. While the use of chlorofluorocarbons in spray cans is banned in the United States, the same does not hold true elsewhere. Should you ever visit or live in another country, refuse to buy aerosol cans powered by the CFCs. At home, take care when handling the food containers and dishware made of the insulating CFC foam. Don't carelessly break them in two or into pieces. Whenever you do so, you add a bit to the destruction of the ozone layer. One broken fast-food cup may not add much to the ozone problem by itself—but the harm is great when several million people break them.

And don't forget to support President Bush's commitment to end the production of all CFCs in the United States by the year 2000.

8. Let the federal government know that you want rigorous steps taken to protect our nation against all types of pollution. When the U.S. Congress is considering an antipollution measure, write to your Senator and Representative and let them know that you support it. Do the same thing when you think that Congress is "dragging its feet" in the passage of needed legislation. And remember that you can also write to your state and local representatives when they are considering antipollution laws. Give your support to all local, state, and national representatives who are working to better the environment.

9. Urge your U.S. Senator and Representative to support the country's participation in international programs aimed at ending all types of pollution. Let them know that you think the United States should play a major role in developing international programs. Our nation ranks among the world's leading polluters and in some instances—the use of the automobile is one—stands as the leading polluter. As such, the United States has the responsibility to spearhead the battle to end global pollution.

10. Finally, as much as you detest air pollution, you must develop a balanced point of view toward it. What is meant here by a balanced view? On the one hand, while you may want all pollution ended, you must realize that its end should not be achieved in ways that destroy the world's industries. They provide vital employment for people everywhere and supply us with many products that we not only enjoy but also need. What must be found are ways by which the atmosphere—and our planet's lands and waters—can be rendered safe again through altering environmentally dangerous practices and procedures but not through destroying industry altogether.

These are just ten steps that, no matter our ages, we can all take to help end not only the poisoning of the sky but all other environmental poisonings as well. There are other ideas that you will surely think of yourself. Should you follow the above suggestions or choose ones of your own, please stick with them. Don't forget them in a few days or weeks. Always remember that, if our sky is to be clean and fresh again, they are steps that *must* be taken.

BIBLIOGRAPHY

BOOKS

Aylesworth, Thomas G. *This Vital Air, This Vital Water.* Chicago: Rand McNally, 1973.

———, *Our Polluted World.* Columbus, Ohio: American Education Publications, 1966.

Battan, Louis J. *Weather in Your Life.* New York: W. H. Freeman, 1983.

Brown, Lester R., Editor. *State of the World 1989: A Worldwatch Institute Report on Progress Toward a Sustainable Society.* New York: W. W. Norton, 1989.

Dolan, Edward F. *Drought: The Past, Present, and Future Enemy.* New York: Franklin Watts, 1990.

Dolan, Edward F. and Scariano, Margaret M. *Nuclear Waste: The 10,000-Year Challenge.* New York: Franklin Watts, 1990.

Dorland's Illustrated Medical Dictionary (23rd Edition). Philadelphia: W. B. Saunders, 1953.

Elliott, Sarah M. *Our Dirty Air*. New York: Julian Messner, 1971.

Environmental Protection Agency. *A Citizen's Guide to Clean Air and Transportation*. Washington, D.C.: United States Government Printing Office, 1980.

Gay, Kathlyn. *Silent Killers: Radon and Other Hazards*. New York: Franklin Watts, 1988.

Hardy, Ralph; Wright, Peter; Kington, John; and Gribbin, John. *The Weather Book*. Boston: Little, Brown, 1982.

Lehr, Paul E.; Burnett, R. W.; and Zim, Herbert S. *Weather*. Racine, Wisconsin: Western Publishing, 1975.

McKibben, Bill. *The End of Nature*. New York: Random House, 1989.

Naar, Jon. *Design for a Livable Planet: How You Can Help Clean Up the Environment*. New York: Harper & Row, 1990.

National Geographic Society, Special Publications Division. *Powers of Nature*. Washington, D.C.: National Geographic Society, 1978.

The 1990 Information Please Almanac. Boston: Houghton Mifflin, 1990.

Sanders, Ti. *Weather: A User's Guide to the Atmosphere*. South Bend, Indiana: Icarus Press, 1985.

Steger, Will, and Bowermaster, Jon. *Saving the Earth: A Citizen's Guide to Environmental Action*. New York: Knopf, 1990.

Weiner, Paul. *Planet Earth*. New York: Bantam Books, 1986.

The World Almanac and Book of Facts 1990. New York: Newspaper Enterprise Association, 1989.

MAGAZINE ARTICLES

Bidinotto, Robert James. "What Is the Truth about Global Warming?" *Reader's Digest*, January, 1990.
Duffy, Michael, and Garelik, Glenn. "A Sizzling Scientific Debate." *Time*, April 30, 1990.
Elmer-Dewitt, Philip. "Preparing for the Worst: If the Sun Turns Killer and the Well Runs Dry, How Will Humanity Cope?" *Time*, January 2, 1989.
———, "L.A.'s High-Watt Highway." *Time*, April 30, 1990.
Gilliam, Harold. "How We Can Fight the Greenhouse Effect." This World Magazine, *San Francisco Chronicle*, July 31, 1988.
Lemonick, Michael D. "Deadly Danger in a Spray Can." *Time*, January 2, 1989.
———, "Feeling the Heat. The Problem: Greenhouse Gases Could Create a Climate Calamity." *Time*, January 2, 1989.
———, "The Heat Is On: Chemical Wastes Spewed into the Air Threaten the Earth's Climate." *Time*, October 19, 1987.
Linden, Eugene. "Big Chill for the Greenhouse." *Time*, October 31, 1988.
———, "The Death of Birth. The Problem: Man Is Recklessly Wiping Out Life on Earth." *Time*, January 2, 1989.
Trenberth, Kevin E.; Branstator, Grant W.; Arkin, Philip A. "Origins of the 1988 North American Drought." *Science*, December 23, 1988.
"Car Pollution Deadline Extended." *Facts on File*, August 13, 1977.
"Environmental Agency Authorized." *Facts on File*, October 1–7, 1970.
"The Heat Is On: Chemical Wastes Spewed into the Air Threaten the Earth's Climate." *Time*, October 19, 1987.

"State of Union Message: Pollution Problem Cited." *Facts on File*, January 22–23, 1970.

"Strong Clean Air Bill Cleared." *Facts on File*, December 17–28, 1970.

TELEVISION TRANSCRIPTS AND SOURCES

ABC News. *Nightline*. "The Environment—Why Should We Care?" Broadcast May 21, 1984.

ABC News. *20/20*. "The Hole in the Sky." Broadcast October 30, 1986.

ABC News. *Nightline*. "Ozone Layer." Broadcast August 26, 1987.

ABC News. *Nightline*. "The Greenhouse Effect." Broadcast September 7, 1988.

NBC. "The Infinite Voyage: Crisis in the Atmosphere." Broadcast January 8, 1990.

NEWSPAPER ARTICLES

Abramson, Rudy. "Bush Urges Action on Global Warming," *San Francisco Chronicle* (from *Los Angeles Times*), April 19, 1990.

Associated Press. "Cost of Proposed Acid Rain Laws," *San Francisco Chronicle*, August 31, 1989.

Brooke, James. "Peruvian Farmers Razing Rain Forest to Sow Drug Crops," *New York Times*, August 23, 1989.

Browne, Malcolm W. "New Ozone Threat: Scientists Fear Layer Is Eroding at North Pole," *New York Times*, October 11, 1988.

Ferrell, J. E. "Acid Rain: The Fallacies and the Facts," *San Francisco Examiner*, July 2, 1988.

———, "Canada, U.S. Face Off in Toxic Border War," *San Francisco Examiner*, July 3, 1988.
Gore, Albert, Jr. "An Ecological Kristallnacht. Listen," *San Francisco Chronicle*, March 19, 1989.
Hazarika, Sandy. "Global-Warming Panel Urges Gas Tax in West," *New York Times*, February 26, 1989.
Mitgang, Herbert. "When Winter Will Neither Chill Nor Charm," *New York Times*, September 20, 1989.
Miyasto, Mona. "Acid Rain Eating Mayan Ruins," *San Francisco Chronicle*, August 13, 1989.
New York Times. "The Environment's Gains and Losses," December 4, 1988.
Passell, Peter. "Cures for Greenhouse Effect: The Costs Will Be Staggering," *New York Times*, November 19, 1989.
Perlman, David. "Scientists Get Set for Polar Mission with New Ozone Warning," *San Francisco Chronicle*, December 16, 1988.
Petit, Charles. "Why the Earth's Climate Is Changing Dramatically," *San Francisco Chronicle*, August 8, 1988.
———, "Ozone Hole Possibly Affecting Australia," *San Francisco Chronicle*, December 7, 1988.
Recor, Paul. "Ozone May Damage Plants, Lead to Food Shortages," *San Francisco Examiner*, September 10, 1989.
Reinhold, Robert. "How Fighting Global Warming Could Be Painless and Profitable," *New York Times*, September 3, 1989.
San Francisco Chronicle. "Global Pollution Pact Signed," November 11, 1988.
———, "Carbon Dioxide Emission by U.S. Sharply Rising," September 16, 1989.
———, "EPA Urges Drastic Action to Slow Greenhouse Effect" (from *New York Times*), March 14, 1989.
———, "U.S. Reveals How Much Industry Pollutes the Air," March 23, 1989.

———, "Bush Seeks Big Changes to Cut Air Pollution (from *Los Angeles Times*), June 13, 1989.

———, "Most Uses of Asbestos to Be Banned by EPA (from *Los Angeles Times*), July 7, 1989.

———, "Bush Clean-Air Plan Unveiled—Critics Say It Has No Teeth," July 22, 1989.

———, "White House Unveils Plans to Study Global Warming," September 1, 1989.

Schuon, Marshall. "Engine Adjusts to Use of Methanol or Gasoline," *New York Times*, December 3, 1989.

Shabecoff, Philip. "Suddenly, the World Itself Is a World Issue," *New York Times*, December 25, 1988.

———, "The Environment as Local Jurisdiction," *New York Times*, February 22, 1989.

———, "An Emergence of Political Will on Acid Rain," *New York Times*, February 19, 1989.

Stevens, William K. "Scientists Link '88 Drought to Natural Cycle in Tropical Pacific," *New York Times*, January 3, 1989.

———, "Ecological Threats, Rich-Poor Tensions," *New York Times*, March 26, 1989.

———, "Culprit in the Greenhouse Effect," *San Francisco Chronicle* (from *New York Times*), November 29, 1989.

Wald, Matthew L. "How the Northwest Asserted Itself on Smog," *New York Times*, June 11, 1989.

———, "Guarding Environment: A World of Challenges," *New York Times*, April 22, 1990.

INDEX

Acid, rain, 3, 4, 9, 16, 39–55
  damage assessment, 48–55
  efforts to control, 99–100
  location of, 41–46
  pH scale, 40–41, 42–44
Adirondack Mountains, acid rain in, 50, 52
Aerosol propellants, 29, 95–96, 98, 110
Antarctic, 2, 24, 26, 27–28, 30
Antipollution efforts, individual, 106–11
Arbor Day, 110
Asbestos, 15
Audubon Society, 108
Australia, 32–33, 36, 72, 77
Automobile exhaust fumes, 2, 4, 11, 21, 71–76
  alternative fuels, 75–76
  catalytic converter, 73–74
  efforts to control, 71–76, 88
  electric cars, 74–75
  laws to limit, 72, 74

Boston, Massachusetts, 2, 11
Brazil, 75, 77
Bush, George, 83, 92, 93, 105, 110

California antipollution laws, 84–86, 90
Canada, 3, 39, 42, 46–47, 50, 72, 79, 95
Cancers, skin, 3, 26, 35–36
Car engine fumes. *See* Automobile exhaust fumes
Carbon dioxide, 3, 6, 20, 59, 60, 64, 65, 73, 76, 83, 101, 102, 109
Carbon monoxide, 2, 11–13, 21, 73, 76, 82, 83
Carbon pollutants, 10–13
Catalytic converter, 73–74
CFCs. *See* Chlorofluorocarbons
Chicago, Illinois, 14, 21
China, 21, 65, 79

Chlorofluorocarbons (CFCs), 3, 9, 27–32, 34, 59, 66, 95–98, 101, 105, 110
　aerosol propellants, 29, 95–96, 98, 110
　efforts to control, 94–98
　emissions, 66
　polystyrene materials, 29
　theory re damage, 31–32
Clean Air Act, 82–83, 84, 85, 90–93, 100
　opposition to, 90–91
Copper Basin, Tennessee, 5
Crop damage, acid rain and, 54–55

Detroit, Michigan, 21
Donora, Pennsylvania, 22
Drought, 67–69

Earth Day, 108–109
El Niño, La Niña, 68
Electric cars, 74–75
Electrostatic precipitation, 78
End of Nature, The (McKibben), 56, 107
Environmental Protection Agency (EPA), 34–35, 43, 83, 84, 89, 99, 100
Europe, western, 39, 43, 65

Federal antipollution efforts, 81–84
Federal Water Quality Administration, 83
Food supply, world's, 37–38
Forest damage, acid rain and, 52–54

Galveston, Texas, 62
General air pollution, 71, 77, 106
　successes and failures, 87–92
Germany, 21, 53

Great Britain, 77, 88
Greenhouse effect, 3, 6, 9, 56–69
　defined, 57–58
　efforts to control, 101–105
　gases, 64–66
　results, 62–63

Halon, 96–97
Health damage, 34–36
　breathing problems, 22
　carcinogens, 17
　eye problems, 26, 34
　immune system, 36
　skin cancers, 3, 26, 35–36
Houston, Texas, 92
Hydrocarbons, 13, 20, 21, 73, 82

India, 72
Industrial burning of fossil fuels, 5, 9, 40, 44–47, 79, 100, 102
　electrostatic precipitation, 78
　scrubbers, 47, 77–78, 82, 99, 100
Industrial Revolution, 7–8
International Union of Air Pollution Associations, 70–71

Japan, 21, 72, 77

Lakes, acid rain in, 50–52
Local government antipollution efforts, 84–87
London, England, 1–2, 5–6, 8, 22, 77
Los Angeles, California, 20, 21, 62, 75, 84–85, 90, 92

McKibben, Bill (*The End of Nature*), 56, 107
Measuring acid rain, 40–44
Methane, 59, 60, 66

Index

emissions, 66
Mexico, 21, 39, 72, 89
Miami, Florida, 62
Molina, Mario J., 21, 32, 94
Montreal Protocol on Substances that Deplete the Ozone Layer, 96, 98, 101

National Acid Precipitation Assessment Program (NAPAP), 51–52, 53, 54, 55
National Air Pollution Administration, 83
New Jersey, 86
New York, 22, 42, 62, 86, 92
New Zealand, 32–33
Nitrogen oxide, 15–16, 20, 21, 59, 60, 66, 84, 101
  emissions, 66, 82
Norway, 72, 95
Nuclear energy, 79–80, 109

Ozone, 20, 25, 84
Ozone layer, 2–4, 9, 20, 24–28, 30–33, 35
  Arctic Circle, 33
  CFC theory, 31–33
  efforts to control, 94–98
  See also Antarctic
Ozone Trends Panel (NASA), 32–33

Pittsburgh, Pennsylvania, 5, 6, 84
Pollutants, 9, 10–23
  carbon, 10–13
  hydrocarbons, 13, 82
  identified, 12–23
  sulfur and nitrogen oxides, 15–16
  suspended particulate matter, 13–15, 82
  toxic substances, 16–19
Pollutants, efforts to control
  American effort, 81–93
  worldwide effort, 70–80
Polystyrene materials, 29, 110

Radioactivity, 17–19
Rowland, F. Sherwood, 31, 32, 94

Scrubbers, 47, 77–78, 82, 99, 100
Seattle, Washington, 62
Sierra Club, 108
Smog, 1, 4, 9, 19–23, 71
South Korea, 72
Soviet Union, 65, 79
State antipollution efforts, 48–87
Sulfur, 15–16, 47, 82, 84, 87, 92, 100
Suspended particulate matter, 13–15, 82
Sweden, 72, 95
Switzerland, 72

Taramura, Alan, 37
Texas, 87
Thermal inversion, 22–23
Toxic substances, 16–19

Ultraviolet radiation, 2–3, 9, 20, 25–26, 33, 37–38

Worldwatch Institute, 64–65, 76, 87, 89

EDWARD F. DOLAN

is the author of more than eighty-five books for young people and adults. Recent titles have had to do with environmental concerns—*Drought: The Past, Present, and Future Enemy* and *Nuclear Waste: The 10,000-Year Challenge* (with Margaret M. Scariano)—but his interests are varied and he has written about sports, space, and social problems, among other subjects. His *Adolf Hitler: A Portrait in Tyranny* was an American Library Association Best Book for Young Adults. His previous title for Cobblehill Books was *Famous Firsts in Space*.

Mr. Dolan worked for many years as a newspaperman and magazine editor. He is a native of California, and he and his wife, Rose, live just north of San Francisco. They have two children, both grown and married.